Bouquet of Dandelions

by Katie Ogeyi Odey

ISBN 978-1-63393-585-3

This is a work of fiction. The characters may be both actual and fictitious. With the exception of verified historical events and persons, all incidents, descriptions, dialogue, and opinions expressed are the products of the author's imagination and are not to be construed as real.

Published by

köehlerbooks™

210 60th Street
Virginia Beach, VA 23451
800-435-4811
www.koehlerbooks.com

Bouquet of Dandelions

Katie Ogeyi Odey

VIRGINIA BEACH
CAPE CHARLES

DEDICATION

To my son, Kenechukwu, and my daughter, Nneka, for giving me bragging rights and reasons to strive to be my best. Also, to my friends for teaching me the value of friendship.

ONE

The rusty autumn evening began to shroud the setting sun. Selma sat in her favorite spot in her townhouse dining room. The contemporary bay window facing the western sky invited Selma to the evening ritual of watching the sunset as her mind wandered. It had been a long day at work, but Selma allowed herself to indulge in the simple pleasure as she sipped some African rooibos tea from a terracotta mug.

The red silk robe she wore fit tight around the hips. After her unsuccessful attempts to lose a few pounds, Selma had settled for her very curvy figure. Having watched her weight fluctuate over the years, she joked about being her own shrink in deciding to stop the dieting cycle. Accepting her curvy image allowed Selma to relinquish the guilt of her painful divorce and the toll it took on her daughter, Kendra.

She gave the mug a gentle shake and waited for the slices of ginger to settle at the bottom.

Selma reflected on her first full work week at the *Uptown Gazette* newspaper with a dash of disappointment because it had not been as eventful as she hoped. Her biggest gig was working with one of the other assistant editors, Jaden Smith, on a story about the opening of the Inter-County Connector, ICC, which was supposed to relieve congestion on the Beltway.

The *Uptown Gazette* had been around for nine decades and was considered the best source for local news around the Washington, DC metro area, despite the popularity of the vaunted *Washington Post.* In Selma's mind, the *Gazette* lived up to its creed—*Excellence in Local News Reporting*—and gave her professional pride. Her satisfaction came from realizing her long dream of being a journalist after a tumultuous divorce from her husband of seven years.

Even in her early college years, Selma convinced herself that teaching was her calling. It meant inspiring young people and enriching their lives, but her passion for reporting the news outweighed even her desire to teach. Montgomery College had given her a good start when she got a job as a part-time faculty member in the English department. Selma wanted and needed more in life than working as an adjunct professor at the community college. She had spent two years seeking a permanent position as an assistant professor.

The position that opened up at the Germantown campus seemed promising at first, but a stronger candidate with more college teaching background got the job. Selma's resume was nonetheless impressive. A Princeton graduate, a master's degree in English and an impressive repertoire of electives in journalism and American history distinguished her. Selma had good reasons to think that her job prospects were great. Although she considered a career that would enable her to use her knowledge of African folklore, the possibility of teaching that subject was very slim. She had excelled in the black diaspora class at the University of Lagos in Nigeria, where she had earned a bachelor's degree in English Language and Literary Studies.

Selma's motivation to study American history came from her fascination with the post-Civil War era. An invitation to a civil rights workshop at the Smithsonian in Washington sparked her interest in journalism. The thought of black journalists being persecuted as they did their jobs haunted her. Writing for a progressive local paper seemed like a perfect start.

"Mom, what's for dinner?" Kendra said as she sprinted downstairs toward the kitchen.

"Check the refrigerator. We have some leftover chicken fettuccini from last night," Selma replied, unperturbed and staring into the distance as darker clouds began to eclipse the now faint sunrays. She took another sip of her tea and continued to look toward the distance.

"Not that baked chicken again," Kendra whined. "Could we order pizza instead?"

"Not today, Kendra." Selma rose to go into the kitchen, but she stopped at the door, watching Kendra as she rummaged through the refrigerator. A punctured can of evaporated milk fell to the floor. Selma walked towards the pantry, taking no notice of the spill. Kendra took out the Tupperware containing chicken fettuccini and placed it on the kitchen counter.

"There is nothing to eat," Kendra complained.

"There's chicken and pasta," Selma responded. Her unflinching constancy had been built up over eight years as a single mother. This type of exchange had become a norm. Her main focus was to create a sense of stability for Kendra after what seemed like an endless divorce. A bitter custody battle made it even more challenging for Selma, and Kendra took full advantage of the situation. Although Selma did her best to ignore Kendra's countless guilt trips, it was hard to ignore the accusation that Selma was responsible for her dad's return to Nigeria. Being the typical strong-willed child, she was not afraid to speak her mind, and Selma would end up playing defense during their power struggles.

"I am tired of chicken and pasta," Kendra fussed, as she slammed the refrigerator door and headed back upstairs. Selma placed her mug in the sink and went into the living room. She had mastered the art of ignoring Kendra after explosive episodes like this. She sank into the sofa recliner and raised her feet.

Selma took her mind away from the strife with her daughter by thinking of topics for her next column. She could write about people going through mid-life crises, baby boomers, children, and retired seniors.

Selma was primarily hired to write a weekly column on popular social issues. Her other job was to work with one of the assistant editors on editorials and feature stories. The short episode with Kendra made her realize the intricacy of writing a column for women in their forties, and the challenges they faced in their personal and professional lives. The easy part was going to be tapping into her personal experiences and those of some of her friends, but the question on her mind was how to write without sounding stereotypical. Many women over forty were married, some not so happily married. Others were trying hard to hold onto families plagued by problems of money, power, and infidelity. Others were separated or divorced, while still others were holding onto careers and learning to define themselves.

Kendra came downstairs and made her way into the kitchen. Selma pretended not to notice her. Kendra's action confirmed her thoughts about what to write about.

Selma's supervisor, Gary Steinberg, was already sold on

the idea of writing for a well-defined audience. He seemed enthusiastic about the column. Gary had a rare position, serving as both a writer and editor of other feature columnists. He'd vet their story ideas and then read their work before submitting it for publication.

Gary had a broad following in the Washington area. He was a renowned satirist who poked fun at the policy makers on Capitol Hill. He had been focusing lately on the debate about the sagging economy. Capitalizing on the dilemma of overspending, taxes, unrest in the Middle East, and the weakening economy, Gary wrote about the US's increasing debt to China. He did not spare members of either party. Selma tried to think of specific ideas that would excite Gary. She was building a list of pitches when Kendra called out.

"Mom!" Kendra shrieked from the kitchen. Selma jumped out of the recliner and rushed into the kitchen. Kendra was holding the handle of Selma's terracotta mug in her right hand and the cup in her left. Selma stared at the pieces of her broken mug on the floor. "I took it out of the sink to put it the dishwater, and I accidentally dropped it." Selma shook her head and turned to leave. "I'm sorry, Mom; it was an accident."

Selma walked back into the living room without saying a word. Kendra let out a deep breath as her mother stretched out on the sofa. She followed and stopped a few steps from the end of the coffee table, her misty eyes staring directly at her mother. Selma looked away for a moment and back at Kendra. There was a teardrop.

"This is what happens when you make an unnecessary fuss," Selma said.

"I didn't mean to break your mug," Kendra whimpered. "It was an accident."

Even though Kendra seemed contrite, she knew she shouldn't have been eating over the kitchen sink. Selma had warned her about that, but Kendra was defiant. “Place it on the counter for me,” Selma replied. “I may be able to glue it.”

“That’s a good idea,” Kendra said, with a bit of a relief. “Do you forgive me, Mom?” Selma beckoned her to sit next to her on the sofa.

“You made your point about not wanting to eat the leftover chicken,” Selma said as she stroked her shoulder. “There is no reason to prove that you are annoyed.”

“Okay, Mom.” Kendra went back into the kitchen.

Selma reached for her laptop beside the sofa. The idea of women in their forties and their constant battles with teenage children, jobs, and expectations seemed like a plausible choice for her article.

At fifteen, Kendra was a typical teenage girl who thought that the world revolved around her. Selma knew she had the materials to write a compelling article. A few other topics came to mind as she contemplated daughters and their relationships with their mothers, and she tried to imagine life with a son instead.

She thought about Lora Clarkson, one of her colleagues at Montgomery College, who was a single mother of three boys. Selma recalled her conversation with Lora, during which Selma had tried to convince her that it is easier to raise boys than girls. Selma talked about her daughter’s sassiness and how, even after almost eight years of raising Kendra by herself, Selma still did feel the mother-daughter bond.

At forty-one, she could not imagine having another child—doing the babysitting juggle, pushing a child on a swing in the park or in a baby stroller. A relationship potentially leading to marriage was very remote, and at her age the prospect of being a new mom was not appealing. She was an active mother and member of the PTA, present at every school band performance, school play, and school lunch date. Yet Kendra would not let her go a day without a guilt trip or two. “You never listen” was a phrase that Selma heard just about every day.

Selma was engrossed in the article she was writing and did not notice Kendra sitting on the other end of the sofa and placing her feet on the coffee table.

"Go ahead, ignore me," Kendra said. "Soon you're going to ask me to help you with your Facebook page, right?"

"I hear you," Selma replied.

"You know I have to babysit for Auntie Christie tomorrow, right?" Kendra said as she leaned toward her mother's computer screen.

It was almost unbelievable that she had grown a few inches taller than Selma and stood at five foot eight—a height difference Kendra relished. Her tall and lanky frame was an obvious reminder of her father.

"Privacy, please," Selma said.

"Did you even hear what I said?" Kendra retorted.

"I know you have to babysit tomorrow," Selma replied, still focused on her article. "I plan to take you to Christie's place before I go to work."

"How are you enjoying your Facebook experience?" Kendra asked lightheartedly.

"Besides it taking too much of my time, I think it's fascinating," Selma replied. She leaned back on the sofa and closed her laptop.

"I don't know what we would do without Facebook," said Kendra. "Seriously, how did you ever survive without Facebook, Instagram, or the Internet for that matter?

"We did not need Facebook," Selma said. "We had more meaningful ways to connect with one another."

"You did not have much of anything during the Stone Age, mom," Kendra teased.

"You are right," Selma replied. "We had better things to do with our time."

The house phone rang just as she placed the laptop on the coffee table. Selma looked at her daughter, who did not seem to notice.

"Could you get the phone for me, please?" Selma asked.

"Who still calls the house phone? Haven't people heard about texting?" Kendra shook her head and rose to answer the phone.

"It's for you, Mom. It's Auntie Christie." Kendra gave the phone to Selma and went upstairs to her room. Selma closed her eyes and shook her head in frustration as she listened to Christie. She paced back and forth as she listened, stopping intermittently to ask her where Martin was and how long he had been gone.

"Mom, have you seen my phone?" Kendra yelled from her room. Selma used her hand to cover the lower part of the phone.

"Kendra, I have not seen your phone, and I'm still on the phone. Can we talk when I get off?"

Selma continued her conversation with Christie. She could already sense that her assurances and admonitions were falling on deaf ears. Christie's fear of ending her marriage was obvious. Her voice echoed through the phone as she complained about her husband's "disappearing acts."

Christie, Selma's best friend, worked as a registered nurse in the Clinical Research Center at the National Institutes of Health in Bethesda. She and Martin had been married for a little over six years, and had a boisterous five-year-old son, Martin Jr. Selma was the maid of honor at Christie's wedding. Thirty-five had seemed like the perfect age for Christie to be married. Selma often blamed her failed marriage on getting wedded in her twenties.

Martin was a successful real estate attorney and the same age as Christie. Tall, with a full head of hair, Martin was the epitome of the handsome rich guy that most women craved. His constant traveling and working late were beginning to weigh on their marriage. Christie would not divulge the full extent of problems she had been having with Martin, but Selma instinctively knew her friend was trapped in an abusive marriage.

Christie was crying on the other end of the line, talking about her recent conversation with Martin, who was once again on a business trip in Las Vegas. Martin had complained about Christie's refusal to travel with him. He told her not to complain about him seeing other women, though he denied having any kind of affair. Sadly, Christie had been left to raise their five-year-old son by herself, while working full time.

TWO

Selma sighed as she ended her call and placed the phone on the hook. The wedding photograph of Christie and Martin on the top shelf of her oak display cabinet caught her eye. Their beaming smiles suggested contentment and pure joy. They seemed perfect for each other. As she looked at the photo, Selma recalled a recent conversation she had with four of her colleagues at Montgomery College.

Five adjunct professors had just finished teaching and were planning in the office one Saturday afternoon. Allen Fletcher, the only male professor in the room, was in his mid-fifties and balding. The youngest of the ladies, Karen Walsh, an unmarried thirty-something Caucasian, talked about the advantages of a woman getting married after thirty.

"Women under thirty are generally naïve and not ready to be married," said Karen. Allen was the first to respond.

"My niece got married at twenty-five, and she is a successful teacher," he remarked.

At some point, the "Hollywood types" got thrown into the conversation.

"We know that young celebrity marriages do not last long," Karen said. "What I find interesting is how they cite 'irreconcilable difference' as the cause of their brief marriages."

Joyce Castillo, the eldest of the three ladies, was quick to point out that the lives of Hollywood types were constantly scrutinized in the media. Joyce pointed out the oddity of some Hollywood couples.

"Thanks to reality shows, they are now airing their dirty laundry," Allen added. He rose and went into the kitchen area.

"What are these people thinking? How do they expect to live normal lives when their lives are reality shows?" Joyce asked in her musical Hispanic accent. "They are living in a fishbowl for the whole world to see."

"That is why they end up in divorce court citing irreconcilable differences," said Allen as he placed his coffee mug on the table.

"When millions of people tune in to watch your good and bad moments, what do you expect?" added Phoebe, a French professor and married mother of two.

"Well, Hollywood marriages are a lot like their movies," Selma added. "They get hyped up and get people's attention, and then it's all over."

"Don't forget the huge settlements," Allen said. "What concerns me is that they tend to trivialize marriage and don't seem to care about how their actions affect their children."

"Well said, Allen," Laurie said. Laurie Jenkins taught remedial English to second language learners. "I believe that most of them decide on a prenuptial agreement because they see the end right from the beginning." Laurie raised her right elbow to cover her mouth while she sneezed.

"Some of them do enjoy blissful unions without getting married," said Allen, with a mischievous smirk.

Selma nodded. "Only Disney fairy tales have 'happily ever after.' I guess the fantasy gives us a reason to cling to the idea of a happy married life," she said, gathering the contents of a big brown envelope to place in her mailbox.

"The ones who decide to have a union without marriage are the smartest of them all," Laurie joked in her trademark dry sense of humor. "They're smart because they have defined their priorities."

Returning to the present, Selma found herself nodding as she picked up the photograph of Christie and Martin, serenely happy on their wedding day, and stared at it. Selma and the three other bridesmaids as well as four groomsmen were all smiles. Selma thought about her friend having to raise a young son and could not imagine chasing an active five year old around at her age.

A text message came in and she grabbed her phone from the coffee table.

Hi sis, just checking in . . . Heading to the airport to fly home tonight . . . will call when I get home.

It was her younger brother, CJ. He had just graduated from Kingston University in London, majoring in computer graphic technology. CJ had worked as an intern for a digital imaging company in south London for two years before he went to college. He decided to go back and work for them after he graduated. Selma sent him a quick note.

I will call you in the morning. She turned off the light and headed upstairs.

Kendra's bedroom door was ajar when Selma got upstairs. She peeked in and saw Kendra sitting on her bed with her laptop on her lap and ear buds plugged into her iPhone. Her school bag was on the floor beside her bed, along with two or three pairs of jeans, sweatpants with the Clarksburg High School logo, and three white T-shirts.

"Where did you find your iPhone?" Selma asked softly. Kendra removed an ear bud and gave her mother an unwelcoming stare.

"Could you knock, please?" Kendra huffed.

"Not when I pay the bills around here," Selma replied. Kendra returned to the Facebook page she had opened. "Kendra, you have not answered my question."

"The phone was in my room, Mother," Kendra said brusquely.

"Kendra, turn off that computer and listen to me," Selma ordered. Kendra pushed the laptop aside and braced herself. Despite her little victories, she clearly understood when her mother would not put up with her shenanigans. "Kendra, nothing gives you the right to be disrespectful to me."

"I'm sorry, Mom." Kendra removed the other bud from her ear and stared at her mother, chin in hand.

"I'm glad you found your phone," Selma said, still trying to exert control. "Is there something wrong?"

"Nothing," replied Kendra. Selma walked in carefully to avoid stepping on the clothes left on floor. She sat on the bed next to Kendra, and for a moment neither of them spoke. Kendra's eyes darted between her mother and her Facebook page.

"Do you still plan to go to the county fair with Nicole this weekend?" Selma asked.

"I am babysitting tomorrow, remember?" Kendra answered in a mellower tone.

"I thought you were planning to go to the fair on Sunday," Selma said.

She could tell that Kendra was hiding something from her. Kendra had the habit of biting and sucking her lips when she was anxious about something. This time, she was not only sucking her lips, she was grabbing her lower lip gently with her upper teeth.

"Oh, you're right," Kendra replied. "I guess I need to call her to remind her."

"Do you think she forgot?"

"Well, Mom, Nicole may not want to go to the fair with me this weekend." Kendra stood up and placed her laptop on her dresser. She adjusted the mirror above her elegant cherry dresser, which was flanked by posters of Taylor Swift and Usher.

"Why?" Selma asked, surprised.

"This is why." Kendra picked up her laptop and sat back next to her mother. She clicked on the page that she had minimized. Selma was speechless as she saw the topless photograph of her daughter's best friend.

"Where . . . where did this come from?" Selma stammered.

"Obviously she sent it to her boyfriend, and he sent it to another friend, who posted it on his Instagram page," Kendra said. "Now it seems like all his friends have been tagged on it and sent it everywhere."

"I've been warning you about the dangers of social networking."

"Some people are just dumb, and they do dumb things," Kendra retorted.

"Don't let me find any ridiculous picture of you on the internet," Selma said.

"Mom, you have Facebook, and you can see what I do," Kendra huffed.

"I don't see everything, Kendra, and you know it," Selma said.

Selma had just joined the bandwagon, even though she still considered Facebook—and the idea of spending hours snooping into the lives of her eighty-three friends—juvenile. She relented after an episode of *Dr. Phil*, who discussed the dangers of predators targeting teenagers through social media. The story of a fourteen-year-old girl, who invited a perpetrator to her home, was enough to convince Selma to create a Facebook account. Using Facebook also enabled her to connect with Kendra on her own level.

When she stood to leave, Kendra returned to her Facebook page.

"I'll drop you off at Christie's on my way to work," Selma said.

"I will be ready, Mom, I promise."

"Good night, Kendra. And be careful. The internet has become a venue for all kinds of nonsense."

"I am not dumb, Mom, and you know it," Kendra retorted. "I will be fine." She let out a loud sigh of relief when her mother finally left.

Selma tried not to show her unease about the half-naked image of Nicole. She shut Kendra's door gently and went to her own room. Her initial thought was to call Nicole's mother, Denise, but imagining Denise's reaction discouraged her. Denise was a single mother of three girls and two boys. Her live-in boyfriend, Orlando, had just been released from jail, where he had served three years for grand larceny and drug possession.

Selma remembered her trepidation the day Kendra introduced Nicole as her BFF during a school talent show. Denise was wearing a loose pair of black sweatpants and Santana Moss's Redskins jersey. Nicole and Kendra were performing a rendition of Michael Jackson's "Black or White" with a group of twelve other girls. Selma recalled how proud Denise was to see her daughter on stage. What Selma found rather bizarre was hearing Denise say that her daughter had "the body to go far in life." Her iridescent, manicured nails and her conspicuous makeup, complete with shiny gray eye shadow, gave Selma the picture of a scared woman seeking attention. The thought of discussing her daughter's half-naked photograph on the internet, and possibly hearing a nonchalant response from the mother, disturbed Selma.

Selma pondered the effects of social networking on younger generations and the impact it could be having on her only child. With so much reliance on the internet, it was clearly an inevitable part of life, yet it had become rather sinister, destructive, and even more mysterious than people realized. For Selma, "the internet woes and woos" seemed like a good idea for her newspaper column. Selma had an uncanny ability to seek and find opportunities in the most unlikely places. In her mind, the paradox of today's social networking technology helping to connect people while creating a destructive environment needed to be sorted out. She would explore social networking sites as breeding grounds for crimes against innocent children.

Selma was eager to go over her lecture notes for her Saturday morning class. She opened the window to let in the cool evening breeze. The polyester curtains swayed, creating a rhythm that captivated Selma for a few seconds. She sat on her bed to work on her laptop and decided to check her email. One caught her attention. The name of the sender was Ursula Adams, and the address was a string of numbers. Out of curiosity, Selma opened it.

She had previously received emails from people outside the US sending bogus requests for money or an account number to deposit a huge "inheritance." This kind of scam not only made news, it became a punch line for late-night jokes. Just like Selma guessed, the sender introduced herself as an attorney whose client was carrying out the death wish of his deceased father. The named client had an inheritance of $4.5 million and needed a trustee to help him claim the funds. This attorney needed a confirmation to deposit the money into Selma's account. There was a $375 fee to expedite transferring the money to her bank account.

Selma junked the email and looked through her college writing textbook to review her lectures. She fought the urge to reply to the scam artists, deciding to focus on her class notes instead.

THREE

Selma parked her green Subaru Forester in front of Christie's lakefront, five-bedroom house on a cul-de-sac in North Potomac. Christie had seen Selma pull up and hurried out of the house wearing her dark-blue scrubs. Her long braids had been put into a ponytail. Selma and Kendra met Christie at her doorstep.

"I hope you aren't too late," Selma called.

"No, I'll be fine. Thank you for coming," Christie said. She was breathing heavily and looked somewhat stressed.

"Good morning, Auntie Christie," Kendra called out as she scurried toward the front door.

"Good morning, Kendra. MJ is sleeping in the living room, and there are cinnamon rolls in the oven," Christie said as she entered 2011 metallic blue Acura MDX.

"Drive carefully," Selma said.

Martin Jr. was sound asleep on the sectional sofa when Kendra walked in. She placed her Redskins string bag at the other end of the sofa and tiptoed into the kitchen. The smell of cinnamon rolls filled the house

"Do you know where she keeps her oven mitts?" Kendra whispered to Selma, frantically opening and closing drawers. Selma's eyes wandered from the stainless-steel refrigerator to the stainless-steel oven and the dining area, which barely had enough space for the extended dining room table, six chairs, and a matching china cabinet. A wooden wine rack had just been installed next to the refrigerator. Three kitchen napkins hung on the side, and next to the napkins were two pairs of oven mitts. One pair was red silicone. She removed the mitts and handed them to Kendra.

"Be careful taking the cinnamon rolls from the oven," Selma warned as she tiptoed back to the front door to avoid waking MJ. Kendra walked back into the living room and sat in the recliner.

"I will see you when I get back." Kendra waved goodbye.

As Selma reached the front door, she glanced at the set of three canvas wall paintings. Christie enjoyed the good life, and she was quick to defend her affluent lifestyle with the expression "the fruits of my labor." She would often say she was living the American dream. Despite the problems she had with Martin, she continued to focus on her job and raising Martin Jr.

Selma felt responsible for letting her best friend marry a man who started abusing her verbally and emotionally less than two years after their nuptials. As much as Selma wanted to blame "the other woman"—in Martin's case, Geraldine Henshaw—for breaking up a marriage, she knew that the person to blame was the man or woman who left the marriage.

Geraldine, an old girlfriend of Martin's, had surfaced less than six months after the wedding. Martin had attended a workshop in New York shortly after Christie found out that she was pregnant. Martin claimed to have bumped into Geraldine at a Manhattan hotel where he was staying. He denied having an affair with Gerry, as he called her, even though they stayed at the same hotel. Gerry had come from Nigeria to New York to attend the Global Women Lawyers Association conference, and it coincided with Martin's real estate attorney's workshop in Manhattan. Selma had her doubts, but Christie believed everything her husband told her.

Geraldine had been Martin's classmate at the Nigerian Law School in Lagos. They had a relationship that Martin claimed was platonic. After Martin won the visa lottery and moved to the US, he kept communicating with Geraldine. As far as Selma was concerned, his marriage to Christie was a marriage of convenience, one that came about because of pressure from family and friends in Nigeria. Although Selma had an inkling about Martin's relationship with Geraldine, she had decided to keep it to herself. Christie believed Martin's story about running into Gerry at the conference in New York and considered their rendezvous as a mere coincidence. Selma made a decision not to probe. She understood how much Christie wanted to hold onto her seemingly perfect family.

Christie was on Selma's mind as she drove down Route 28 toward Montgomery College in Rockville. She recalled the first time she had met Martin. That first impression had not changed. She met Martin when Christie invited a few of his friends, including his best friend, Diola, to dinner at the townhome she was renting in Germantown. Martin's gregarious personality was in full display as he talked about how lucky and blessed he was to have met Christie, a fellow Nigerian. He shared some of the horrors of dating and marrying American women in the past.

"I am not just from Mars. I am Mars; Ares himself," Martin bragged. As if comparing himself to the infamous Greek god of war were not enough, he bragged about his conquests and his expertise in the real estate business. Selma's stomach churned as she listened to her friend's fiancé make disparaging remarks about women. She noticed Diola shaking his head in displeasure. His wife, Yemi, sitting next to him, was startled at Martin's remarks. Christie did not seem to care. She was laughing and nudging Selma. Selma gave her a quizzical look and questioned her taste in men. Even more puzzling to her was how easily Christie dismissed his comments as the silliness of a person who had been drinking.

"Drinking can make you act stupid, but it doesn't mean that you are," Christie told Selma.

"Get a grip, Christie!" Selma scolded.

Martin had indeed consumed three cans of Budweiser that evening and a couple of martinis. Still in total disbelief, Selma excused herself and asked Christie to accompany her to the bathroom. Christie shrugged and cautioned Selma not to read too much into it. When they returned, Christie sat next to Martin like a faithful puppy. That evening, Martin's narcissism had seemed obvious to everyone in the room—except Christie.

Selma pulled into a space in the faculty parking lot and removed her school bag from the back seat. She noticed a text message from Christie on her cell phone: *Sorry I couldn't stop to talk. Thx for bringing Kendra.*

She hurried into the adjunct office to pick up her attendance roster before class. Although she empathized with her friend, a part of her still blamed Christie for not seeing the signs. She remembered calling Christie the day after the party to express concern about Martin's behavior, but Christie dismissed it and assured Selma that he would change once they got married and had children. Her desperation was obvious, but Selma resisted the urge to give further admonitions. Having been married and having a child of her own, Selma understood Christie's urgency. After all, she was a typical African woman, who faced constant scrutiny about marital status.

Christie often expressed her desire to have a child before it was too late. Her biological clock was ticking and running low on batteries. For fear of losing her best friend, Selma had supported her during her trying marriage to Martin.

Selma had been teaching Saturday mornings at Montgomery College for five years, yet it did not make waking up early any easier. She grabbed the roster from her mailbox and headed to her classroom. A few minutes before nine, most of the students had arrived. She looked over her attendance list and noticed that two students were absent: Tyrone Wilson and Gladys Anderson.

Tyrone's absence was not surprising. He had the habit of missing class and complaining about his mother's attitude. He had told Selma on the first day of class how much he despised the idea of going back to school. He wanted to pursue a music career as a rap artist and believed that his mother should support him instead of insisting that he get an associate degree. Gladys, however, was never absent. Selma was a bit concerned about her.

Working as a CNA at Shady Grove Adventist Nursing Home was hard for Gladys, but she hardly missed a class, even when she had a night shift. Selma was surprised to learn that, at thirty-eight, she had a twenty-one-year-old son. Gladys had stayed back after class one day and opened up to Selma about her family. He son had been in and out of prison for drug possession and larceny. Gladys, a single mother, had two jobs and was looking for a third job to support her son and his pregnant girlfriend, who were living with her.

Forty-five minutes into class, Gladys walked in quietly and sat in the empty seat by the door, her tiny braids loosely held together in a pony tail. She wore an oversized green sweatshirt revealing dried ketchup stains. She reached into her backpack and removed her English composition book and a red binder. Selma smiled at her and continued to explain a writing prompt to her class. She noticed some dried tears and knew something was amiss. Both Gladys's eyes were noticeably swollen.

"I am very sorry for being late for class, professor," Gladys said as she handed her homework assignments to Selma after class.

"Is everything okay?" Selma asked, looking intently into her tired eyes.

"Professor, it is getting too much for me," Gladys explained. "I am determined to complete this program and work towards my LPN." Tears rolled down her cheeks. "My son is back in jail, this time for domestic violence."

Selma placed her hand on Gladys's shoulder. The woman started sobbing as she tried to explain the agony of trying to keep her son off drugs.

"He could have gone back to get his GED, but he has refused to do something with his life." She rubbed off her tears with her fingers, and lowered her head.

"I am sorry to hear this," Selma said. "I know you are working hard to better your life."

"It is hard when you work hard and things fall apart anyway, professor." Gladys's sobs grew louder. Selma gave her a hug. The lingering odors of tobacco and a hint of Icy Hot ointment were overwhelming. Gladys had told Selma that she was trying to quit smoking—unsuccessfully.

"I am sorry," Selma whispered again.

"Thank you, professor," Gladys said. "I should be heading to the hospital now."

"Who is sick?" asked Selma.

"My son's girlfriend, professor," Gladys replied. She tightened her lips and closed her eyes for a brief moment.

"What happened to your son's girlfriend?" Selma asked. "Is she okay?"

"No, professor," Gladys replied. "She went into labor after the big fight she had with my son last night." Selma patted her on her shoulder.

"I hope things work out for you, Gladys," said Selma. "You are a strong woman."

"Thank you," Gladys said. "Thank you for listening."

The two women parted, Selma heading for the department building, and Gladys for the bus stop across the street.

Just before leaving the building, Selma's phone vibrated. A text message had just come in from Kendra. *I need batteries for my calculator . . . and can I have a Big Mac from McDonald's?* The phone rang just as she was about to reply. It was Julie, her former lawyer and current friend.

"Hi, Julie."

"Selma, I hope your class is over, and I'm not calling at a bad time."

"No. You're good. Class is over."

Selma sometimes stopped at Julie's house after her Saturday morning class. Julie was calling to find out if Selma was coming. Selma told her that she was heading to Christie's house to pick up her daughter.

"Why don't you join us at Christie's house?"

"I would rather not," replied Julie. "I don't like being around Martin, you know."

Julie had a reputation for being blunt. It seemed to have served her well as a family law attorney. The two met when Selma was divorcing her husband of six years, Eric Bawa. Julie was the chief attorney for a non-profit legal firm that represented women who were victims of domestic violence.

Julie had given Selma the hope and confidence she so desperately needed. There seemed reason to expect a David and Goliath showdown when Julie agreed to take her case. Julie took pride in being referred to as a courtroom brawler. The two women had an instant connection.-

"Too many women endure all kinds of abuse, and it needs to stop," Julie told Selma on the first day they met some seven years earlier. "Some women are afraid to leave their abusers because they feel helpless. I have made it my mission to change that and offer women hope, and I hope I can do that for you."

Selma had fought back tears as she listened to Julie. Almost twelve years of verbal and emotional abuse from Eric had become too much. She recalled Eric accusing her of being an unfit mother because she did not teach Kendra their language or culture. The last straw came when Eric threatened to take Kendra to Nigeria to live with his mother.

Julie understood Selma's ordeal. The first consultation became the start of a friendship that would last beyond the duration of Selma's case.

On the day of Selma's first court appearance, Julie marched into the courtroom rolling a small black briefcase behind her. With an African-American father and a Mexican mother, Julie had a smooth, toffee skin and a full head of curly, dark brown hair that came down to her shoulders. She wore her signature black four-inch heels, which complemented the petite, dark-gray Ann Taylor suit. Selma had smiled with confidence when she saw her attorney. Julie looked poised and ready for a court battle.

Julie worked tirelessly to help Selma retain the townhouse. Three months into the case, Selma received a call from the sheriff's office while she and Kendra were visiting her aunt Serena, in California. There had been a house fire. Since her home was one of the newer ones in the housing development, the sprinklers minimized the fire damage, but most of her belongings were destroyed.

There was a pink sheet taped to the door when Selma and Kendra returned. The charred window frames and rooftop were visible from the street corner. The city had deemed it uninhabitable, since the main structure had been severely damaged by the water used to douse the flames. Kendra asked Selma if she could go in to get her jewelry box. Selma had pointed to the sign on the door. She shook her head and closed her eyes to let the tears fall. She was surprised that Kendra remained calm even when she could not go into the house to get her belongings.

Selma and Kendra had moved in with Laurie Jenkins, a fellow adjunct professor at the college. Selma salvaged a few items of clothing and some pots and pans when a deputy sheriff escorted her back to the house the following day. She purchased some secondhand clothing and cooking utensils to live a modest life with her colleague. Her computer had been destroyed, but it was not a total loss because she still had most of her important materials on a flash drive.

The fire was ruled as arson. Knowing how vindictive Eric was, Selma knew that he had made good on his promise to make her pay. Eric acted surprised and indignant when Selma confronted him outside the courtroom about the fire. His apathy shocked everyone, including his own lawyer. The real shock came when he announced his plans to move back to Nigeria right after the judge admonished him to play an active role in his daughter's life.

Julie continued to represent Selma even after she joined another law firm—Matthews and Allen, a firm well known in the DC metro area. Three months after the case, Selma and Julie had met at IHOP for brunch. Julie did not seem surprised when Selma informed her that Eric had returned to Nigeria and married another woman.

"What a bastard," Julie remarked, and explained that it was a strategy to avoid paying child support or alimony. She invited Selma to lunch at her Rockville home, and the lunch turned into a routine.

At forty-two, Julie had never been married. Her devotion to her job and the countless hours she spent preparing for her cases left very little time for any kind of social life. She had dated a fellow attorney two years earlier, but the relationship ended after five months.

Julie agreed to meet at Christie's house once she was sure that she did not have to deal with Martin. Selma hung up and sent a quick text to Kendra before she got into her car.

FOUR

A red Honda Pilot was parked in Christie's driveway when Selma arrived. Kendra rushed to open the door.

"Hey, Mom," she said as she ran outside. "Did you get my Big Mac?" Selma reached into the back seat for two McDonald's meals. "Thanks, Mom," Kendra said, rushing back into the house.

"The other one is for MJ," Selma said. "Does Auntie Christie have visitors?"

"Two of her friends stopped by, and they are making some Nigerian fish soup," Kendra replied as she took a few fries out of the bag.

MJ was playing with a set of Star Wars Lego pieces on the coffee table. Kendra gave him one of the bags. Two ladies sat at the kitchen table while Christie stirred the soup in a stainless stockpot. The unmistakable aroma of black peppercorn and ginger filled the kitchen and the living room.

"Hello, ladies," Selma said, dropping her bag in a chair and joining the women in the kitchen. "Habibah, it's been a while.

How are you doing?" Habibah wore a yellow tie-dye dress that accentuated her shiny dark completion.

"Fine, my sister," Habibah replied, before remarking, "Kendra is a big girl now."

After winning a state beauty pageant in Nigeria at the age of eighteen, Habibah became an instant celebrity, and enjoyed the fame that came with it. In spite of the controversy arising from being a Muslim contestant in a beauty pageant, she was adamant about showcasing the true beauty of a Muslim woman. Two years later, she denounced her religion and declared that she was agnostic. Despite her age, Habibah was still a beautiful African woman, with deep dimples, flawless skin and tall, languid curves.

"They grow up fast," said the pregnant lady across from Habibah. She wore a loose caftan embellished with gold embroidery on purple silk.

"Selma, I don't think you have met Afi, my friend and co-worker," Christie said, giving the soup a quick stir and joining the women at the table.

"I have heard a lot about you," said Afi to Selma.

"Good things, I hope," Selma said. MJ ran into the kitchen holding two broken pieces of one of his action figures.

"Mom, Darth Vader is broken," MJ whined. Christie took the broken toy from her son and followed him into the living room.

"He stepped on it by accident," Kendra exclaimed in his defense.

"Let's talk to Daddy about it," said Christie. "He will get you a new one." Christie could see how distraught MJ was about his broken toy. He eyes quickly filled up with tears as he looked at his broken toy and at his mother. "Your dad will get you another Darth Vader," Christie reassured.

"How far along are you?" Selma asked Afi.

"Thirty-three and a half weeks," Afi answered softly.

"She will be popping out a bouncing baby boy for her American hunk of a husband," Habibah joked. Afi laughed. "You know you have arrived in the US of A when you marry a handsome white man."

"I don't think it matters who you choose to marry," said Selma. "What matters is that the man treats you with respect."

"*R-e-s-p-e-c-t*," Habibah sang, mimicking Aretha Franklin. Christie turned off the stove and went back into the living room. Kendra was watching the show *Drake and Josh* on Nickelodeon while MJ played with a new superhero toy, Buzz Lightyear.

"Kendra, why don't you take Junior downstairs?" Christie told Kendra. It was a welcome offer for Kendra, who was getting uncomfortable being around her mother and her friends. Her mother talking about a man treating his wife with respect got her attention. MJ gathered his action figures and headed down to the basement.

"Auntie, may I use the computer?" Kendra asked.

"Yes, you may," Christie said.

"Thank you, Auntie Christie." Kendra hurried downstairs.

"What a polite child," Afi said to Selma. "You raised her well, Selma."

"I am glad you saw this side of her," Selma said with a slight grin. She took some soup bowls out of cabinet above the dishwasher and placed them on the kitchen counter. Afi stood and asked to use the bathroom.

"The powder room is on the left side of the front door," Selma said. Afi stood for about a minute admiring the luxurious furniture and paintings in the family room. She was struck by a painting of an African woman with a child on her back, carrying a clay water pot before a backdrop of a fading sun on the horizon. She pondered the hardship of rural African women who were expected to care for their children and cater to needs of their family. The sofa-sized painting hung above an electric fireplace. A black bag containing Martin's golf set was next to it.

"These people sure love a good life," Afi said under her breath as she closed the bathroom door behind her.

"I need to go to the basement to get the baby stuff for her right after we eat some pepper soup," Christie said. Selma looked surprised.

"I told Afi that she could have my baby furniture and some other baby items that MJ is not using. I am not planning to have any more babies," she declared.

"Are you really sure about this?" Selma asked. She recalled Christie telling her how much she would like to have a baby girl, so it was rather strange that she was giving up the idea of having a second child.

"Very sure," said Christie. "Don't you need a man in the house to make babies?"

"Well," Habibah interjected, "sometimes you have to do what is best for you."

There was an eerie silence. Selma squeezed her lips and shrugged slightly. Again, she could not help feeling responsible for the turmoil in her friend's life. She regretted not questioning it from the beginning, yet she had considered the possibility of destroying their friendship. Her own failed marriage was enough reason to want her best friend married and happy.

Habibah's cell rang. The ringtone was Tina Turner singing the chorus of her signature song, "What's Love Got to Do with It." All eyes were on her as she rummaged through her zebra-print handbag for the phone. Selma nodded to the rhythm. Christie stood and swayed her hips, singing the lyrics as she opened the pot of soup and let out some steam. Selma joined in off key and swayed as she brought one more soup bowl out of the cabinet and placed it on the counter next to the stove. Habibah found the phone a few seconds after the song stopped. Afi stepped out of the powder room and closed the door behind her. There was a knock on the door.

“I should have told you, Christie,” said Selma. “I spoke with Julie earlier and invited her here.”

“The more the merrier,” Christie said. There was calmness in her demeanor, and she seemed to enjoy the company of her friends. Selma went to the door as Afi made her way back to the kitchen.

“Hi, everybody,” Julie said, hugging Selma, who was still holding the door handle.

“Julie, I am so glad you could come,” Christie said. “We are all here in the kitchen.”

“This is turning out to be a girls’ day out,” Habibah remarked. “Can I help with the drinks?”

“Sure, look in the refrigerator,” Christie said.

Habibah opened the refrigerator and stood still for a moment, letting her eyes wander, trying to decide what drink to get. At the back of the first shelf was half a gallon of Arizona Iced Tea behind a box of Splash Cooler Capri Sun. A bottle of California sparkling wine was tucked at the back of the first shelf. She took out the cranberry juice.

The ladies all sat at the round kitchen table, each holding a glass while Habibah filled them. Christie poured the hot soup into the bowls that Selma had placed on the counter.

“Please make mine small,” said Julie. She didn’t hide her obsession with her healthy diet. Christie brought a small bowl of soup for Julie. “Smells delicious,” she exclaimed as she pulled it towards her.

“Is it too spicy?” asked Christie.

“Pepper soup is not for the faint of heart,” Julie said. She took a sip and reached for her glass of cranberry juice. Selma smiled, recalling the day she invited Julie to her home for fish soup. Julie had surprised her when she ate up the soup and did not seem to be bothered by the spiciness. In Selma’s mind, Julie had the guts to withstand just about anything, even a steaming bowl of African spicy fish soup. For her part, Julie respected Selma's determination to succeed in her career—Selma exemplified the old saying that whatever does not kill you makes you stronger, and Julie had expressed how much she admired Selma's tenacity.

"How is your work at the *Uptown Gazette*?" Habibah asked.

"My first week went well," Selma said.

MJ ran upstairs, stumping his feet and yelling. "Mom, Kendra won't let me watch *SpongeBob*," he cried.

"He has been watching *SpongeBob* all this while, and he doesn't want me to change the channel," Kendra said as she marched upstairs close behind MJ.

"Kendra, MJ is a child, and you know better," Selma scolded. "This is his house and—" The Westminster chime from the Bulova Norwood Pendulum clock interrupted her.

"He is a spoiled brat," Kendra said.

"MJ, you need to remember that Kendra is your guest," Christie said.

"I will just go on Instagram and let him watch what he wants," Kendra said, and returned to the basement.

Christie's countenance changed for a brief moment. Despite her calm demeanor, she was very protective of her son. But she stopped herself from reacting to Kendra's comment about MJ.

As an only child, MJ was used to being the center of attention. Even though Kendra babysat him and was close to Christie's family because of Selma, MJ had a hard time sharing, and Christie had to walk a fine line with Kendra, whose reactions to criticism could be unpredictable. Like MJ, Kendra was an only child. More importantly, Christie needed Kendra to babysit MJ. With Martin out of town two and sometimes three days in a week, she was forced to make a more permanent babysitting arrangement. She was able to sign MJ up for before and after-school programs, but she needed Kendra to take care of him each weekend that she had to work. She was also careful with Kendra because she valued Selma's friendship.

"Children!" Habibah exclaimed.

"I have tremendous respect for all mothers," Julie said. "Every one of them!" She glanced at Christie with unquestioning admiration. "You need to have a truckload of patience to deal with them."

"You have to double that dose of patience if you are a single mom," Habibah concurred. Selma nodded. At thirty-nine, Habibah had a twenty-year-old son. Her final year of high school had been marked by an unplanned pregnancy at nineteen.

Shortly after Habibah's mother died of breast cancer, her life took a drastic turn that led to an affair with a married man—Mr. Bengha, her father's best friend. During the last few weeks of her mother's life, Mr. Bengha offered Habibah the moral support that she needed to care for her. Her father expected her to do all the cooking and domestic chores. Six months after her mother's death, as Habibah was fully assuming the role of her mother and helping her siblings cope with the loss, her father was killed in a freak accident while riding his motorcycle on a dirt road. Her aunt came to help whenever she could, but Habibah became solely responsible for her siblings.

Mr. Bengha became indispensable during the months following her father's death. Habibah blamed herself for getting pregnant with Mr. Bengha's child. Although Mr. Bengha accepted the child, he remained devoted to his wife. His wife was a registered nurse, who was living and working in the capital city. She came home on weekends and holidays.

Habibah carried the baby to term three months after graduating from high school. She decided to go into nursing as the quickest way to find a stable job. Mr. Bengha's support started to dwindle after she graduated from nursing school. With the responsibility of taking care of her own siblings, she was forced to take a part-time job at a private clinic to help pay for her brother's college expenses.

The idea of leaving the country and starting a new life elsewhere, possibly in America, appealed to Habibah; after all, she had been forced to make decisions that would affect her siblings. Her prayers were answered when she won the American visa lottery, more commonly known as a green card. She sold a few of her belongings and gathered her brothers together for a family meeting at her one-bedroom apartment.

The city of Jos was not too far from her hometown of Akwanga where the youngest of her three brothers, Gowon, was rounding up his associate degree program at the state Polytechnic. Her other two brothers, Omar and Rashad, were attending the University of Jos, Omar majoring in sociology and Rashad a law student. Habibah had been the driving force for her family, working two jobs to support her brothers and her son. She informed her brothers that she and her son were moving to the United States. The news did not come as a surprise. Her brothers had always seen her as a strong, hardworking woman with a pragmatic outlook on life and an unmistakable drive to succeed.

"I am enjoying this girls' day out," Christie said. "Why don't we make ourselves comfortable in the living room?"

Selma helped Christie put the bowls in the sink while the ladies made their way to the living room. MJ's videogame in the basement was getting louder.

"Selma, you were going to tell us about your new job at the *Uptown Gazette*, right?" Habibah asked.

"Well, my first week went well," Selma said. "You know how it is in the corporate world."

"Yup, you start from the bottom," Christie said. "As a woman, sometimes you have to tolerate a whole lot of nonsense to make it to the top."

"There are certain things that I simply won't tolerate," Selma said confidently.

"At our age, we don't have to tolerate too much," Habibah concurred. "I believe that at forty we have paid our dues."

"Amen," Julie said, raising her half glass of cranberry juice. "I have seen too many men, mostly husbands of my clients, who think that the world revolves around them."

Julie and Selma often joked about the lecture that the judge had given Eric, when he considered himself the boss of his family. The judge rebuked Eric for his callousness and reminded him that even he, a judge, was raised to respect women.

"Hey, Habibah, you are not forty yet, you know?" Selma joked.

"I will be in four months," Habibah responded, raising four fingers to stress her point. Afi smiled, rubbing her stomach and giving Selma a fleeting look as if she expected her to say something about Afi's age.

"My supervisor has been very supportive so far," said Selma. "I just want my own column. I know exactly how I want to write it."

"It is time we assert ourselves and help others to rise above their circumstances," Julie affirmed.

"Julie is right," Christie responded. "You are now in a very good position to dole nuggets of truth to women, and help them realize their self-worth."

Selma nodded.

"I agree with you and Christie, Selma," Julie remarked. "Also, you have to be passionate about the issues you choose to write because they will make a difference."

"For so long, we have been pushed to the bottom of the pile," Habibah added.

"So true," Afi concurred.

"With all the insidious reality shows pervading our lives these days, there is definitely a need to focus on real-life issues for a change," Julie added. "That is why we need you to write about things that we care about."

"Who knows, you could be the next Oprah on TV, focusing on people like us," Afi remarked.

"Absolutely," Habibah said.

"If you think about it, not many of us have the passion to pursue our dreams," Afi added. "All it takes is for someone like you to inspire us and make us realize that we can if we try."

"I am already feeling the pressure," Selma said. "That is why I want to focus on women our age."

"What a great idea," Habibah said. "There is a lot to say about women in their forties besides cosmetics that promise to keep us young forever." Christie and Julie laughed raucously. Afi stood, holding her stomach, and headed for the bathroom again.

"Let's face it, we are at an age where we see a mid-life crisis heading towards us like a raging bull, and menopause is creeping in the back door," Selma said.

"Then we find ourselves trapped between menopause and mid-life crises," Christie added. Julie laughed.

"Let's not forget that some of us have to face family issues on our own," Habibah said.

"Single moms, singles—or whatever terminology they use these days," Julie said.

Habibah took a quick glance at her. Julie continued, "I know that I don't fit into the single-mom mold, but I have met so many in my practice that I can honestly empathize with them." Selma nodded, giving Julie a look of approval. Being the only woman in the room who had never been married and did not have a child, Julie was visibly concerned about the wary look on Habibah's face.

"Well, maybe we need to think seriously about getting back into the dating game," Habibah said, turning her attention to Selma.

"Some of us have been there, done that," Selma responded, glancing at Julie.

"Men our age don't seem mature enough to handle women who have it together," Julie replied.

"Sometimes I think that men are afraid of successful women," Selma said. "That may be the reason why they get intimidated by women who have careers and are ready to compete for higher status."

"In my practice, I have seen men who are intimidated by their wives' success," Julie said.

"Don't you think it is unfair to say that about all men?" Afi asked.

"Afi is right," Habibah admonished. "We all have to realize that our experiences are all different."

"Trust me, I have been on a few dates," Julie said. "I go out with men that I consider enlightened, but guess what? They show their insecurities and craziness in no time at all."

"Maybe if you find the right person, things will be different," said Afi.

Julie cast a boorish glance at Afi. Her mind immediately went to a recent date she had had with Sam Hayward, a colleague at her former law office. He had acted like a perfect gentleman, opening the door politely, holding her hand and helping her out of his two-seat Mercedes Benz when he dropped her off at her condominium complex. Two days later when she called him, he did not answer. The following week when she ran into him at the court lobby, he waved sheepishly at her and got on the escalator.

Selma tightened her lips and glanced at Julie. Afi understood. She smiled at Selma, giving her an approving look. Here she was, an African woman from Ghana in her late thirties, married to a Caucasian man, who worked as a DC lobbyist. Logan Fisher had spent two years in Ghana as a Peace Corps volunteer and fallen in love with this beautiful daughter of the local chief. Their marriage resulted from a fortuitous meeting at her father's compound, when Logan came to present a report on the clean water project he was helping to organize. Afi helped interpret what Logan was saying to the elders. One week later, she went on a date with Logan.

"I will be the first to admit that there are a few good men, black and white and in between," Julie said. "You just have to be lucky to find a good one."

"Afi's husband, Logan, is a very good man," said Christie, looking at Afi for approval.

"I agree," replied Afi. "He treats me well, and I have no doubt that he loves me dearly."

"Now you see why I want to write my own column?" Selma said. "Issues about women or people our age seem endless." She paused. "Think about it, I could talk about family life, raising children, maintaining relationships, dating, and the list goes on."

"As a journalist, you have to experience some of these issues too," Christie said, with a mischievous glance. "You know, like dating."

"Well, the club scene is not for people like us," Habibah responded, coming to Selma's defense.

"There are some decent clubs out there for reasonable people," Julie remarked.

"How about online dating?" asked Christie.

"This is the twenty-first century after all; everything is done online these days," Selma said.

"So, would you consider online dating?" Julie said. "It's about time, Selma."

"I am still trying to find my way around Facebook," Selma

joked. "Hey, but this journalist is not afraid to try anything." She sipped her cranberry juice and crossed her legs.

"That's my girl," Julie replied. She raised her hand and gave her a high five.

"You know all three of us are in this together—you, me and Habibah—right?" Selma said.

"Well, we need a brave soul like you to take the lead," Habibah joked.

"So, what seems to be the problem here?" Christie asked. "You are all classy women who cannot be intimidated."

"If you see a dating website where there are real men with class, please let us know," Habibah said with a smirk.

"We cannot give all men a bad rep," said Afi. "There are men with class out there. I know because I married one."

"I totally agree with Afi," said Julie. "You know what they say: 'One bad apple spoils the bunch.'"

"Now I know I will have a lot of fun writing my column," Selma said. "We have spent all this time talking about men, and I am thinking about a headline like, 'What women say when they talk about men.'"

"That will be one to read," said Julie. "Yup, I am that curious." She laughed.

"And know men who will read and talk about it," Habibah said.

The house phone rang, and Christie stood to answer.

"I got it, Mom," MJ yelled from the basement.

Selma stood up as well and walked to the window. Darkness was setting in quickly. Christie went to the basement while the ladies watched the evening news on Channel 4. Christie emerged carrying two large plastic bags full of baby clothes.

"You could have the crib as well," Christie said as she placed the bags on the floor next to Afi. "You'll need a truck to haul the crib and changing table."

"Thank you so much," Afi said. Julie stood and took a quick stretch.

"Are you certain that it's a boy?" Julie asked. Habibah grinned and stood as well.

"I can tell that it's a girl," Habibah said with a confident look.

"Well, I hope you are wrong," Afi replied. "I am scheduled for another sonogram in two weeks, and that should confirm the gender of the baby."

"It's time to go," Selma said.

"We should do this more often," Christie responded. She moved the bags to the door for Afi.

"Thank you for having us," Julie said.

Kendra emerged from the basement holding her Redskins drawstring backpack. The crisp autumn chill was present, and the ladies felt its sting as they made their way to their cars. Christie dragged the two bags of baby clothes to Habibah's Honda Pilot. MJ ran barefooted to Selma's car.

"Goodnight, Kendra."

"Goodnight, MJ," Kendra replied. Christie held MJ's hand and waved to her friends as each zoomed off. Afi rode in Habibah's car. Christie and MJ made their way back to the house.

FIVE

Selma woke to the sound of sirens. It was not uncommon to hear sirens in Clarksburg so early in the morning considering the congestion. The traffic did not bother Selma much since her house was adjacent to the shopping center and about a quarter of a mile from busy Route 355. Selma's church was three miles north on Fredrick Road.

The clouds were thickening as Selma made the ten-minute drive to church. The meteorologist on Channel 4 had talked about some scattered thunderstorms, but there was no sign of rain or drizzle. Selma took her usual seat at the back, close to the emergency exit. The padded pews had just been upgraded to red wooden chairs to match the red carpet.

Sunday morning worship at Gateway International Community Church in Clarksburg was a mix of evangelical and Episcopalian with a contemporary style that included classical hymns and music from singers like Chris Tomlin. Selma had been attending the church since she moved to Clarksburg. Kendra enjoyed the youth program, which was the main reason Selma decided to call Gateway her home church.

Ms. Edna sat in the seat adjacent to Selma's. She hugged Selma during the interlude following the sermon. Known for her effervescent personality, Ms. Edna always ended her greeting to parishioners with "Ain't God always wonderful." Her pale skin showed obvious signs of aging around her neck and upper arms. Selma smiled and patted her shoulder. She caught a glimpse of Rosie Hilton and her family sitting two rows away. Selma stayed focused on Reverend Jim Ballenger's message on mustard-seed faith. The allusion of trust as the catalyst for faith resonated with Selma because she wanted to believe that there was indeed a greater power that she could learn to trust.

Rosie had been the first person to greet Selma the first day she attended Gateway. Silky blond hair brushing her shoulders, she introduced herself as the wife of one of the deacons, Kent Hilton. Her daughter, Ashley, and Kendra were born two months apart. The girls became friends almost immediately. They had sat together in the front pew, and Kendra could not wait to call Ashley when they got home. Kendra was disappointed to learn that Ashley was homeschooled. Selma drew conclusions about the Hilton family following a conversation with Rosie after church that first day. She played it back in her mind.

"I am glad Kendra is making friends with Ashley," Selma had said as they walked toward the parking lot.

"Me too," Rosie replied. "I wish they went to the same school."

"What school does Ashley attend?" Selma asked.

"She is homeschooled," Rosie had replied bluntly. "I had to pray about my decision to quit my job and homeschool Ashley." She noticed the bewilderment on Selma's face. "I am not comfortable with the idea of Ashley attending public school."

"Please help me understand," Selma said. "Why don't you want her in a public school?"

"I don't want to offend you, Selma," Rosie said. "They have

teachers with questionable backgrounds." She paused and waited for a response. Selma gave her a blank stare and then tried to force a smile through her tight lips. Rosie stepped closer. "The curriculum does not include materials and instructions that I consider important to my family."

"I guess that's your choice," Selma said.

"I have a master's degree in clinical psychology, and I had a good job with the county's Health and Human Services," Rosie explained. Selma took a lazy step towards her car as Rosie continued. "My husband's salary is enough to sustain our family."

"Where does your husband work?" Selma asked.

"He is a pediatrician," Rosie had replied. "If you or your friends need a pediatrician, I'm sure he's still taking new patients."

"I will keep that in mind," Selma said. Although she had doubts about being Rosie's close friend, she admired her friendliness.

Sunday service had gone on without any major excitement. Pastor Ballenger's words about active faith resonated with Selma. "Active faith requires a definite action," the pastor preached. "It requires stepping out in faith, knowing that God will honor your obedience to him." As she walked out with the other parishioners, Selma felt a renewed determination to make the best of her column.

The clouds turned ominous shortly before noon. Selma and Kendra felt big drops of rain as they walked into the house. Selma sighed with relief when she saw the downpour through her kitchen window. Even above the sound of pouring rain and a few rumblings of thunder, Kendra could be heard chatting with Ashley on the phone. Selma did not want to bother her about lunch. She warmed up some leftover orange chicken and ate at the kitchen table.

A copy of the *Washington Post* was still in its plastic wrap. Selma had subscribed to the Sunday edition because she was interested in the magazine inserts. The front-page headline caught Selma's eye: *The Supreme Court Ruling on Obamacare.* The photograph of protesters on both sides showed a great divide on the comprehensive healthcare reform proposed by President Obama. She skimmed through the article while she ate her lunch.

"Mom, Auntie Christie is here," Kendra called, sprinting down the stairs in her Clarksburg Coyote pants and T-shirt.

"How do you know?" asked Selma.

"I saw her car from my window," Kendra said as she hurried toward the front door.

"There is leftover orange chicken in the refrigerator," Selma said, putting her dish in the sink and following Kendra. Christie got out of the car slowly, grimacing in pain. Her braided hair was loosely gathered in a ponytail. Selma opened an umbrella and rushed out to meet her. Selma saw that Christie's left eye was bruised and swollen, and Selma's puzzled expression quickly turned to rage. Christie managed to smile, but her pain was obvious.

"Don't tell me!" Selma's voice was low and threatening as she channeled Xena, warrior princess. "Martin did this to you." Christie nodded and walked into the house with Selma, each step excruciating. Selma shut the door just as the wind picked up.

"Hi, Auntie Christie," Kendra said as she headed back to her room. She had learned early on not to be around when there was a crisis with Christie.

Selma opened her side-door freezer and removed a plastic icepack while Christie tried to make herself comfortable on the sofa. It was not the first time Martin had assaulted her physically. Selma placed the icepack gently on Christie's forehead and sat next to her on the sofa. She noticed a slight bruise on her friend's elbow and touched it.

Christie groaned and Selma took her hand off.

"What happened?" Selma asked.

"He came home shortly after midnight, and when I asked about his workshop, he did not want to talk." Christie pulled herself up slowly. "I asked him if he had seen Geraldine again, and he snapped. Then—" She started sobbing.

"Then what?" Selma asked. There was a rumble of thunder as the rain intensified.

"Then . . ." Christie hesitated. "Then I confronted him about Gerry, and asked him if he had been with her."

"And?" Selma asked, staring directly at Christie like a police detective.

"He slapped me across the face and punched me in the head." A flood of emotion ranging from disbelief to rage churned up in Selma. Although she realized that she could not blame herself for letting Christie marry Martin, she could not suppress the guilt she felt for supporting her best friend despite her doubts.

"Have you had anything to eat today?" Selma asked.

"I am not hungry," Christie whispered.

"You need to eat something, and then we'll figure out what to do," Selma said before heading into the kitchen. The rain tapered and dark clouds began to dissipate quickly.

"I told you I'm not hungry," Christie said.

Kendra came downstairs and joined her mother in the kitchen. She glanced at Christie, who was beginning to doze off on the sofa.

"Is Auntie Christie okay?" Kendra whispered.

"Shh!" Selma removed the orange chicken, still in its original container, from the refrigerator. After dishing out the food, she placed it in the microwave. Kendra held the refrigerator door for almost a minute before taking out a bottle of water. Christie was waking up when Kendra tiptoed into the living room. She smiled and whispered, "Hi, Auntie." Selma brought the plate of orange chicken and a glass of water and set them on the coffee table. Christie sat up gingerly, placing her hand on her forehead. Selma thought about making another attempt to ask her what happened, but she decided to focus on helping her feel better.

"I brought you some water," Selma said softly.

"Thank you, Selma," Christie replied and cleared her throat. "I have a throbbing headache." She opened the bottle and took a sip. Selma noticed the redness in her left eye.

"You need some Tylenol or Advil," Selma said.

"Advil, definitely," Christie replied. Selma went back to the kitchen to get the medicine for Christi. Kendra was already in the kitchen eating some orange chicken.

"I didn't see you come back in," Selma remarked.

"You were talking with Auntie Christie," Kendra replied. Selma took the bottle of Advil out of the cabinet above the refrigerator.

"Mom, why can't we get a dog?" Kendra asked. She had wanted a pet ever since taking care of the neighbor's beagle. The elderly man's wife recently passed away after a long battle with ovarian cancer, and while she was in the hospital, Kendra walked the dog every day.

Despite that show of responsibility, Selma was skeptical that her daughter would take care of a pet full time.

"You know taking care of a dog is a huge responsibility," Selma said.

"Mother, I told you I'll take care of it," Kendra retorted.

Kendra pouted, finished eating, and returned to her room without another word. Selma turned her attention to her friend.

"Christie, you really need to think about what you want to do," Selma said. "I mean, you just can't continue like this." She gave her the Advil.

"What am I going to do?" Christie replied. She could not conceal her helplessness. "I feel trapped, Selma."

"You're not trapped," Selma scolded. "You have to decide if you want to continue getting black eyes from a man who cares nothing about your welfare or if you want to take charge of your own life."

"Selma, what will happen to me, and to MJ?" Tears rolled down her cheeks. Selma tried to fight back her own tears.

"I know I am not a counselor or an expert on marital affairs," said Selma, "but I know that Martin was never right for you." A weight seemed to lift from her shoulders when she finally said what she wished she'd said the day Christie met Martin.

"What do you mean?" Christie asked.

"I saw the signs from the onset," Selma said. "Martin wants a trophy wife, that's all."

"You mean he doesn't love me?" Christie was not ready to hear this.

"I am saying that you deserve better," Selma said. "If he really loves you, why does he hit you?" Selma paused. "It is not okay for him to hurt you like this."

"No marriage is perfect." Christie adjusted the icepack on her forehead. "I cannot leave him; MJ needs both of us."

"And I want the best for your family," said Selma. "Only you can decide to stop this cycle of abuse or continue to accept it." Selma rose and went into the bathroom.

"Telephone," Kendra called from upstairs.

"Who is it?" Selma asked.

"Uncle Martin." Selma came out of the bathroom holding a small mirror. Christie's lips trembled as she mouthed "What?" She rose up gently, still holding the icepack on her forehead and taking painful steps towards the kitchen.

"Where are you going?" Selma demanded as she walked past Christie into the kitchen to pick up the phone. Her eyes transfixed on Christie, Selma answered. "Yes, she is here," she replied to Martin coldly. Christie stood at the door. The color of her light brown face faded like wilted autumn leaves. "Do you want to speak with her?"

Selma handed Christie the phone. They walked back to the living room, and Christie dropped the icepack and sat in the sofa. Sitting across from Christie, Selma could hear the anguish in her friend's voice as she uttered faint yeses and occasional nos.

Martin was famous for his charisma and charm. He would almost certainly talk Christie into going back. Selma could not understand Christie's devotion to him in spite of his infidelity and disrespect. She understood the sentiments that Christie's family members and friends had, and she understood that what folks at home thought was important to her friend. Being married and staying married was all that mattered to Christie.

Martin had alluded to Selma's divorce when he made a disparaging remark to her one week after his wedding: "A good woman would do whatever it takes to keep her man and stay married." He went on to point out how American culture destroyed African marriages. Selma recalled telling him that his remarks did not warrant a response and walking away. Martin had often insinuated that his wife was better off with friends who were actually married and had intact families.

Christie ended the call brusquely and handed the phone to Selma.

"He wants you back, right?" Selma asked with a stare that questioned her intelligence.

"Yes," Christie replied sheepishly.

"I guess calling the authorities to report his abuse is out of the question," Selma said. "You don't need to tell me what he said. I am sure Martin does not want you to tell me anything."

Christie looked defeated and said nothing.

"Of course, he's sorry, and he wants you back so you can be a family," Selma continued.

"Selma, you don't understand," Christie retorted.

"Of course, I don't understand. After all, my own marriage failed, so I couldn't possibly understand! Listen, you are one of my best friends, and you have become like a sister to me."

"So are you saying that I should not go back to my husband?"

"I am not telling what you should or should not do," Selma replied, stressing every word. "I care about your welfare, and I want, more than anything, for you to be happy."

Christie went to the bathroom, and Selma went back to the kitchen and picked up the newspaper from the counter. She diverted her attention to her column. Christie's situation had added one more idea. She thought about women like Christie, who were trapped in abusive relationships and too fearful to leave.

Christie came out holding the melting icepack to her eyes.

"Your eyes are still swollen," Selma said calmly. "You need to do something about them."

"I know what you are trying to tell me, Selma," Christie said. She paused. Selma's lip tightened as she stared at Christie. "I can't imagine a better solution than to go back and make things right." Christie shrugged. "Maybe we will go to counseling eventually."

"And you expect Martin to go to counseling, right?" Selma could not hide her displeasure and disbelief at Christie's naivety. "For goodness sake, Martin will not change who he is."

"I don't know, but I'll try," replied Christie. "Maybe I'm the one that needs to change."

"What are you afraid of, Christie?" Selma asked. "Losing your big house and your fancy possessions?"

Christie was sobbing softly, but Selma remained stoic. She stood and walked to the window. "It's your choice to let him walk all over you."

"Stop it, Selma," Christie snapped.

"The truth hurts," Selma said as she sat in the chair across from Christie. "Only a person who cares deeply about you would tell you the truth. I care about you and your little boy."

"You have a strange way of showing it, Selma," Christie cried. Selma moved next to Christie.

"I'm sorry that I am so hard on you," Selma responded. "Having gone through my own problems, I would not wish it even on an enemy." She patted Christie on the back. "You and MJ will be fine, but you need to stay strong for both of you."

Christie wiped her eyes and nodded. "I think I should be going home now." She picked up her purse and her keys and headed for the door.

"Take care, Christie," Selma said as she opened the door and waited for Christie to leave. She thought about walking her to the car but hesitated. She stood at the door and watched Christie get into the car still showing signs of pain. She closed the door and leaned back on it for a minute. Selma then hurried to her room to work on her pilot article. She had to decide whether to continue with the topic of raising teenagers and the obstacles women face doing it, or to explore the poor choices women make because they fear uncertainty and failure.

As a divorced woman, she considered the notion that readers of her column would interpret her article as an endorsement of divorce. However, the obligation to give a voice to other women who were abused weighed more heavily on her. As a rookie journalist, she understood that she would be judged for her content, style, and objectivity.

She could allude to the appearance of advocating divorce by writing a piece that would challenge women in their forties to refuse to be defined by careers and marital status. Her goal was to awaken women's consciousness to the idea of the *trophy wife* and to urge them to refuse to be contented with the idea of being their husbands' prized possessions. Her ideas flowed quickly, with a rhetorical question as her lead.

Do women have the right to be themselves in their pursuit of happiness?

With this, Selma wrote about the desire of successful women to assert themselves, while appealing to others who, in her opinion, accepted unfavorable situations in failing marriages just to save face or, at the very least, conform to the expectations of a "happily-ever-after" life that existed only in fairy tales. As a conclusion, Selma used a quotation from Virginia Satir: "We must not allow other people's limited perceptions to define us."

SIX

Selma walked briskly into the *Uptown Gazette* offices with a renewed sense of confidence. Dressed in a gray Anne Klein suit, black blouse, and Aerosole shoes, Selma trotted towards the building holding her leather briefcase. She thought about Christie but did not let her anger overwhelm her. Instead, she focused on what she hoped to accomplish and what would, perhaps, become the platform of her journalism career.

Selma had worked on her article until midnight and went to bed satisfied with her decision to use Christie's story as a doorway into the fear of uncertainty that sometimes kept women trapped in unhealthy relationships. Her boss, Gary, was talking to one of the security officers stationed at the entrance when Selma walked in through the rotating door.

"Look who's here," Gary exclaimed as he extended his right hand to shake with Selma. "Great to see you bright and early, Ms. Griffin."

Gary's jovial personality was the first thing Selma had noticed when she came for her interview. He was jovial, of Italian decent, balding and almost sixty with a well-trimmed mustache and a slightly protruding midsection. He often quoted Marlon Brando's famous line in *The Godfather* movie, saying "I'm gonna make you an offer you can't refuse." It was exactly what he told Selma that first day, and he did, in fact, make her an offer she could not refuse.

"Good morning, sir," Selma replied and shook Gary's hand.

"I hope you have met Spencer. Spencer Green is one of our security officers," Gary said heartily.

"We haven't been introduced yet," Selma said, reaching out to shake Spencer's hand. "It's nice to meet you, sir." Spencer smiled and accepted her hand. Selma's politeness impressed him.

"The pleasure is all mine, ma'am," he replied in a husky tone. He was tall with a noticeable southern accent. He was one of four African Americans whom Selma had met at the *Gazette* so far.

"Are you ready to take on your second week at the *Gazette*?" Gary asked.

"As ready as can be," Selma replied with a confident smile. She walked through a big common area surrounded by offices of the staff writers and assistant editors. The conference room was between two of them. A photograph of the newspaper's owner hung in the conference room along with a plaque rendering the first front page of the *Uptown Gazette*. Gary and the editor in chief, Steven Blackwell, had offices at the back of the conference room.

Selma's cubicle had the basics: a computer, color laser printer, a cherry-stained desk, and a file cabinet. Her first order of business was to print hard copies of her draft for Gary. She quickly retrieved her article from the flash drive and printed two copies. Her cell phone chimed. It was a text from Kendra. Although it was not unusual to get texts from her daughter, this was rather early and raised some concern. She sat down and read the message.

Mom, can I go to Ashley's house after school today? Kendra was supposed to have informed her about her plans before she left for school. Selma sent a short reply: *Busy now, will text later*. She picked up the papers to head to Gary's office; there was another text alert. She ignored it and left.

Gary was leaning back in his black leather executive chair when Selma arrived. He had been reading and making editorial marks on the front page of the *Gazette*. His desk was huge and L-shaped with plenty of space for his computer and widescreen monitor. The laser printer was on a shelf next to his desk. Selma noticed a family portrait on his desk. There was another photo of two young men with a lady in the middle. An enlarged photograph of a toddler was on his front wall next to a framed diploma from the Columbia University Graduate School of Journalism. On the back wall, he had an elegant antique picture of the Coliseum in Rome.

"You have been working very hard, Ms. Griffin," Gary said, leaning forward. Selma smiled.

"I just want to do my best, sir," she replied. "Thank you for the opportunity . . . You have a beautiful family."

"Thank you, Selma," Gary said. "I still don't know how I got so lucky to have these wonderful people in my life." Selma was still standing. "Do you have a minute?"

"Of course I do, Mr. Steinberg," said Selma.

"Enough with the pleasantries!" Gary exclaimed. "Why don't you sit down and tell me about your article."

Gary read the lead and skimmed through the first few paragraphs. "I find it intriguing that your idea originated from the situation with your best friend."

"My ultimate goal is to write stories that I can vouch for and articles that emanate from relatable experiences." Gary nodded in approval.

"Remember that your job as a journalist is to make sense of

the complexities of life and report what you see," Gary explained. "You have to figure out your style and run with it."

"Thank you, Gary," Selma said. She smiled when she noticed a glossed wooden plaque with the inscription of the First Amendment above his door.

"As soon as you find your niche, you will be okay, kid." Selma nodded. As she rose to leave, a fax came in, and Gary rolled his chair toward the printer to get it.

"Thank you, Mr. Steinberg . . . Gary," Selma said. "Thank you for believing in me."

"You are okay, kid," Gary said. "Do you have an extra copy for Jaden? I want him to give this a second read. Jaden's one of our best assigning editors, and you'll be working closely with him."

"Yes, sir. I have a copy here. I'll bring it to his office right away."

Selma left and headed to Jaden's office. He was in the main area talking with a photographer about a breaking news story. A deranged gunman was holding up one of the county offices.

"I will be with you shortly," Jaden said. Selma waited outside Jaden's cubicle, letting her eyes wander the office space. There were numerous pictures of newspapers around the room. The one that caught Selma's eyes was a front page of an old faded newspaper with a pair of glasses placed on. Jaden returned to his office with an urgent look on his face.

"I should be helping with the article you are working on," said Selma. "What would you like me to do?"

"Take your time to get acquainted with the *Gazette*," Jaden said as he sat down and faced his computer. "I understand that you had to work on your pilot article." Selma nodded.

"I understand that you are working on that breaking news story in downtown Silver Spring," Selma said.

"Yes, a gunman . . . May be a hostage situation." Jason replied. "If you don't mind, I'll take a look at your draft as soon as I finish posting what we know on our website."

"Let me know what I can do to help," Selma said. "I'll be at my desk."

"You bet," Jaden replied. "I may need you to help us chase this story. I'll be heading down there shortly. Hang loose."

When Selma arrived at her cubicle she noticed four more texts. They came from Kendra. She had just started typing a text message to Kendra when Jaden appeared. Working in a cubicle without a door was something Selma had to adjust to. With the intensity of the news business, having privacy in a busy place did not seem like a necessity.

"We need to make a quick dash to downtown Silver Spring to get a few interviews for our article before we run it," said Jaden.

"Sure," Selma replied. "I just need to send a quick text to my daughter."

"No problem," Jaden replied and left as quickly as he came. It was no time to get into a power struggle with Kendra. She simply typed, *Okay. Just let me know when you get there.* She closed her document and pulled her dark sunglasses from her bag. A freckle-faced college intern had joined Jaden.

"CJ, have you met Ms. Selma Griffin?" Jaden asked.

"Not formally," said Curtis. "I'm Curtis Jenson." He extended his hand and shook Selma's.

"So that's where the CJ comes from," Selma said. She noticed the dark green dragon tattoo on his right wrist.

"Yes," CJ replied.

"I'm Selma," Selma smiled. "My younger brother's name is CJ." Curtis beamed, his green eyes fixed on her.

"I look forward to working with you, Ms. Griffin," Curtis replied. "Your brother must be very proud of you."

"We are taking my car," Jaden announced. They got into his 2014 Honda Accord, Selma in the front passenger seat and Curtis in the back. As they drove out of the parking lot, Selma thought about being the oldest in the group. She had to choose between feeling old and having enough energy to keep up with staffers ten to twenty years her junior.

There were other news reporters at the county building when they arrived. Jaden instructed Selma and Curtis to interview one or two eyewitnesses or family members before making his way into the building to talk to council members.

The gunman had opened fire and wounded at least two people before being apprehended. He was a low-level office worker who had been fired and was out for revenge.

The three staffers returned at 2:45 PM and wrote the article in Jaden's office, sending the draft to Gary half an hour later. The goal was to have the article written and edited before 5:00. Updates had been posted online throughout the day and then the complete story would print in the morning paper.

The experience of being on deadline was exhilarating. The best part of Selma's day was being able to interview a family member of one of the wounded victims.

"My wife is one of the lucky ones," a man had told Selma. "She got hit in the arm, but, thankfully, she'll be okay." The quote was included in the article.

A text from Kendra interrupted her thought. *Mrs. Hilton is bringing me home.*

Selma typed, *Okay*, and then spent the rest of the afternoon editing her article before she left the office for home.

Selma opened her front door and took off her shoes before dropping her briefcase on the sofa. Kendra was still at Ashley's. The house was eerily quiet. Selma stretched out on the sofa. It seemed like a perfect time for reflection.

The house phone rang, and Selma reluctantly stood up to answer it. It was Christie's home number. Christie's voice was muffled. With the cordless in hand, Selma walked back to the sofa.

"What?" Selma asked.

"Afi's husband got shot at work today," Christie said, her voice trembling with distress.

"How is he?" Selma asked. She did not wait for an answer before she asked about Afi. "How is Afi?" Kendra walked in, and Selma put her finger on her lips to shush her.

"Hi, Mom," Kendra whispered. Ashley and Rosie Hilton waved as they walked in after Kendra. Selma waved back.

"Hi, Rosie, hi, Ashley," Selma said with her hand over the phone's mouthpiece. "Please excuse me, I have to take this call, but I will be with you in a few minutes." Selma retreated upstairs.

Rosie sat in the chair and crossed her legs. She was wearing a pair of white jeans and a cotton tunic. Her finger and toe nails were perfectly manicured, with a glossy dark pink showing through her four-inch heel sandals. Her eyes wandered through the house as Kendra and Ashley paced the kitchen.

Selma's overall impression of Rosie was not good. She found her to be cynical and ostentatious. Rosie had a smug superiority and was quick to talk about her master's degree in psychology. Selma remembered her mother telling her that people who felt the need to show who they were and what they possessed actually hoped that others did not notice what they were lacking.

Selma recalled the day Rosie told her about her choice to homeschool. She had emphasized that being a mother took precedence over everything else, and she did not seem to think that any teacher was good enough to educate her child.

The sound of shattering glass broke the silence.

"Are you okay?" Rosie called out. Selma hurried to the kitchen with the phone still in her hand.

“Let me call you back,” Selma said. “I will stop by after dinner.” She placed the phone on the counter and tiptoed around the broken drinking glass.

“I’m sorry, I broke your favorite glass,” Kendra said as she swept the glass with a long broom.

“Just make sure you don’t step on it,” Selma said. “Ashley, please be careful, okay?” Selma joined Rosie in the living room.

“Hi, Rosie,” Selma said.

“Hi,” replied Rosie. “It was very kind of Kendra to come over and help Ashley with her history project.” Selma looked puzzled. “We started discussing the Civil War, and Ashley needed to research the states that helped to preserve the Union.”

“We have completed that unit in US history,” Kendra said proudly.

“Did you finish your research?” Selma asked Ashley.

“Yes, ma’am,” Ashley responded.

“I need to show Ashley something in my room,” Kendra said.

“Fine,” Selma responded. “Can I get you anything?” she asked Rosie.

“Some cold water would be fine, thank you.”

Selma went back into the kitchen and returned with a bottle of water and a glass.

“How are things with you at the *Gazette*?” Rosie asked as Selma sat on the sofa across from her.

“Fine. Busy first day.” Selma paused. “I helped to report on the shooting at the county offices.”

“It must be exciting to get involved with current events and write about them,” Rosie continued. “I heard about the Silver Spring shooting.”

“It was crazy,” replied Selma.

Kendra and Ashley joined them in the living room.

“We should be leaving,” Rosie announced. She stood gingerly and adjusted her blouse around the waist.

"Thank you for dropping Kendra off," Selma said, as she walked towards the door.

Selma hurried to the phone as soon as she walked back through the house. She called Christie, and there was no answer. Christie answered the second time Selma called.

"Have you heard from Afi? How is her husband?" Selma inquired. She whispered, "Thank God," when she heard that Afi's husband was alive and would be okay.-

It seemed odd at first that Selma would be so worried about a person she barely knew, but when she thought about being at the scene of a tragic event, she could not imagine writing a news story about the death of someone she had become acquainted with. "Thank you, Christie. I'll plan to stop at your house tomorrow, and we can go and visit her."

SEVEN

By 8:45 PM, Selma was ready to go to Christie's house. She checked her phone and found the text Jaden sent an hour and a half earlier. Their article had been published on the *Gazette* website. Selma could hardly contain her joy when she saw the double byline, *Assistant Editor Jaden Smith and Staff Writer Selma Griffin*. Selma had a long way to go to prove herself and felt she was off to a solid start.

Determined to bask in her little success, Selma called Julie, the one person who rooted for her and reminded her that she could accomplish great things. In some ways, Julie saw Selma's success as her own. She often encouraged her female clients to thrive and make the best of their lives after their divorces, and she had conscripted Selma to use her life's story to inspire other divorced women. Just as she expected, Julie was overjoyed when Selma told her about the article.

"I'm sorry to spoil this moment, but I need to tell you that Afi's husband was wounded in that shooting," Selma said.

"How is he now?" Julie asked.

"I'm about to find out," Selma replied. "I'm heading over to Christie's house in a few minutes."

Selma ended the call and grabbed her keys from her dresser. Kendra was sitting on her bed and writing in a notebook.

"Why don't you ever do your homework at your desk?" Selma asked.

"This is how it works for me, Mom," Kendra replied nonchalantly.

"I need to head over to Auntie Christie's house," Selma said. "I will be back soon."

"Are they fighting again?" Kendra asked in a sarcastic tone.

"No," Selma replied firmly. "Make sure you finish your homework and go to bed on time."

Weekday mornings were stressful for Selma because Kendra fussed about waking up too early and complained about the school bus driver, who she said was grouchy. With Selma's new job, she had to leave at least half an hour before Kendra. She was concerned about Kendra waking up and getting to school on time, but she had to trust that Kendra could handle the responsibility. After realizing that her mother would not drive her to school because of her new job, Kendra learned to get ready and ride the bus to school. Selma called Christie to inform her that she was on her way.

The security lights in Christie's driveway lit up as Selma pulled in.

"Thank you so much for coming," Christie whispered and led Selma into the house. She was wearing gray sweatpants and a T-shirt. Her braids were tied into a pony tail.

"How are you doing?" Selma whispered. She was sure that Martin was home.

"Better," Christie said. "I am very worried about Afi."

"What's his condition?"

"It's critical," Christie said. "Afi is at the hospital, and I am afraid she could go into premature labor." Christie's lips trembled and her voice cracked.

"I'm here now," Selma said. "Would you like us to check on her today?"

"I told her that I'd see her today, but I was waiting for you," Christie replied. A strong feeling of guilt washed over Selma, and she wished she had been more compassionate toward Christie.

The first time Selma noticed a bruise on her arm, Christie told her that she had fallen down the stairs. Selma was not convinced that she was telling the truth; however, she expected Christie to be honest about what was going on since she had taken on the role of a friend and a big sister. Selma remembered the backlash and the loneliness she felt during her separation and divorce from Eric, and she understood why Christie would cover up the mistreatment by her husband. Christie had not talked about the fight she had with Martin since she left Selma's place, and Selma did not expect her to call to let her know how things were. After their disagreements, Christie would double down on her role as a dutiful wife who must not share what was happening in her home. At that moment, Selma understood how much Christie needed her.

"We better get going if we want to get to the hospital tonight," Selma said. Christie got her purse from the bottom of the stairs and removed her keys. Thankfully, there was no sign of Martin. They rode in Christie's car and arrived at the hospital ten minutes before the end of visitation hours. Christie walked up to the information desk and asked for Logan Fisher's room.

"He is in the intensive care unit on the third floor," the attendant said. "Visiting time is almost over, and only very close family members are allowed to see a patient in the intensive unit."

"I understand," Christie said and leaned slightly on the counter. "I am a nurse myself. My friend is like my little sister, and she needs me."

"Okay. He is in Room D-317."

Selma and Christie hurried into the elevator to the third floor. Afi sat in a chair next to the bed and held her husband's hand, stroking it and raising it to her face. Logan had a bandage around his head and was hooked to an IV machine; a heart monitor beeped continuously. His face was swollen and his eyes were shut. A larger tube inserted in his mouth was connected to the third machine. Afi started sobbing when she saw Christie and Selma. Selma patted her gently on her back.

"I am sorry to see you go through this," Selma said. Christie noticed a summary chart on the shelf. *Gunshot to the head, point of penetration 11cm from the temple. Patient remains sedated.* At the bottom of the sheet in bold letters it read, *No liquid or solid food, intravenous fluids only.*

"Have you had dinner?" Christie asked.

"I am not hungry," Afi replied. Christie held her hand and walked her out of the room. Selma, joining them, gently pushed back one of Afi's braids that was hanging loose.

"Afi," Selma whispered, "I cannot even imagine what you are going through right now, but you need to take care of yourself." Afi sank into Christie's arms and sobbed.

"Think about your baby," Christie added as she patted Afi gently on her back. Afi nodded and took a quick glance at Logan through the glass. "Why don't we take you home, and I'll call Habibah to come by your place and stay with you for the night."

"I have to be here with him," said Afi. "I cannot leave him now." She pulled away and took another glance at Logan,

"You will be back tomorrow," Selma reassured her.

"What if—" Afi sobbed.

"Nothing will happen," Christie interjected. Afi went back inside and took Logan's hand. Nothing had changed. The beeping of the heart monitor brought a sense of relief. She kissed his forehead gently and removed her bag from the shelf next to his bed.

The ride home was quiet. Selma's mind wandered back to the shooting and how she worked on the story with Jaden, not knowing that the story would hit so close to home.

"Did you hear any details?" Selma asked, breaking the ten-minute silence.

"I got a call from his secretary that there was a shooting," Afi said. "He was heading back to Capitol Hill for a hearing about a bill he helped to lobby for, but he found himself face to face with the deranged gunman as he left his office." She began to sob again.

"Take heart, Afi," Selma said as she pulled into Afi's parking spot at her condo complex in Rockville. Christie had been on the phone with Habibah, who was making the twenty-five-minute drive from her home in the Flower Hill area of Gaithersburg. Afi walked up to the second floor breathing heavily. Selma took a quick glance at Christie as Afi opened the door and walked into the dark apartment. Christie flipped on the light switch behind the dark brown leather recliner and helped Afi sit in it. She dropped her keys on the coffee table and went into the kitchen. As she rummaged through Afi's refrigerator looking for a quick meal for her, Selma took out her phone to check the time. The photograph of Afi and Logan in matching African brocade caught Selma's attention for a brief moment.

A short while later Habibah walked into the apartment.

"My sister, we thank God for everything." Habibah said.

"I found some leftover lasagna," Christie said. She brought a Pyrex glass storage container from the bottom shelf.

"Don't worry, I will take it from here," Habibah said.

Christie and Selma left and were soon pulling into Christie's driveway.

"Selma, I really appreciate you going to see Afi with me," Christie said. "I hope you know how much I value our friendship."

"That's what friends are for," Selma said. Her attention turned to the door, where Martin came out in his blue silk striped pajamas and stood with arms akimbo.

Christie got out of the car and hurried to the door while Selma headed for her own car. Christie said a faint "Hi" as she tried to squeeze past Martin. He brushed her aside and hurried towards the driver side of Selma's car.

"You are not married. Christie is," Martin yelled. "You can gallivant or do whatever you choose, but you must leave my wife out of it."

Selma turned off the car engine and leaned forward on her steering wheel, giving a Martin a look of disgust.

"Martin, there is a lot I want to say to you right now," Selma said. "But you are not worth it." She turned on the engine.

"Leave my property before I call the cops," Martin thundered.

"Martin," Christie screamed.

"Get back in that house," Martin snapped. Selma shook her head as Christie obeyed.

"You are a narcissistic spoilt brat, and I refuse to dignify your childish rants with a response," Selma said and pulled out of the driveway. The last thing she heard was him calling her "loser."

On the drive home, she flashed back to the reaction she had when she watched the performance of Oliver Goldsmith's play, *She Stoops to Conquer*. She remembered wondering what it would take for women to be more assertive and more independent.

EIGHT

Selma got to her office shortly before eight the next morning. Arianna and Lisa were at their desks when she arrived. She picked up a copy of the *Gazette* from the desk in the hallway. The lead headline was *Deranged Gunman in Downtown Silver Spring*. She glanced at the double byline and smiled. She recalled Martin's assertion of her as a loser and wished he were there to see her article.

A tall brunette wearing a stylish blue dress walked into the office adjacent to Jaden's. "It's nice to have you back, Cynthia," Arianna said. Cynthia returned the warm welcome with a broad smile. Dark red lipstick enhanced her full lips and added glamour to her professional look. Jaden stopped by Selma's office when he saw her enter.

"Great job on your first article," he said.

"Thank you, Jaden," said Selma "We make a great team." Cynthia called Jaden's name. In spite of the stressful nature of news writing and reporting, the *Gazette* prided itself in having a welcoming work atmosphere.

"Welcome back, Cynthia," Jaden called back. He walked to Cynthia's cubicle and gave her a hug. Selma wished she could be part of the pleasantries. She was a staff writer after all. She stepped out of her cubicle, smiling and looking around. She exchanged glances with Cynthia, who was now standing outside her office.

"Selma, please come and meet Cynthia Bridges, our chief foreign correspondent," said Jaden. Cynthia shook Selma's hand and smiled, revealing a slight dimple on her left cheek.

"It is really nice to meet you," Selma said.

"Selma is our newest staff writer and a budding features columnist," Jaden said.

Selma smiled.

"Welcome to the *Gazette*," Cynthia said. "How do you like it so far?"

"I love every minute of it," Selma replied.

"It's another fine day for news," Gary said.

Selma returned to her office and placed her phone on her desk. Her mind went to Logan. She looked at her phone, hoping for a call or a text to update her on his condition. Gary knocked on the side panel and walked in.

"Ms. Griffin," Gary said, "you are a contender." Selma knew he was referring to her article.

"Thank you, Mr. Steinberg."

"Well, since we are on a last name basis, Ms. Selma, I mean Ms. Griffin, I should let you know that you have a meeting with Mr. Blackwell," Gary joked. Selma chuckled and shook her head. At that time, she realized that Steven Blackwell would have the final say about her column. The only real contact she'd had with him was at the interview. She had sensed his reservations then. He was the only person who mentioned Selma's accent.

Selma had nineteen unread emails. She quickly opened Steven Blackwell's email that read, *Hello Ms. Griffin, I had a chance to read your pilot article, and I would like to meet and talk with you some time tomorrow.*

Jaden also sent an email informing Selma that they needed to check out a developing story in the Associated Press regarding a congressman from Idaho who had been involved in racketeering and misappropriating campaign funds to pay for extravagant trips abroad. Selma opened the Associated Press page to pull up the story.

There was an email notification from Curtis about a breaking story in Gaithersburg. Selma opened it as a new tab to read the about a house fire in Montgomery Village.

She noticed Mr. Blackwell walking to his office and decided to see him before going over the story. She printed a copy of her pilot and placed it in a manila folder before heading over.

A brass plaque with Steven Blackwell's name and title engraved in bold letters hung beside his door, which was ajar when Selma got there. She knocked and waited.

"Come in, Ms. Griffin," Mr. Blackwell said in a deep, husky voice. Two manila folders lay on his huge L-shaped mahogany desk. His computer and printer were on the right side of the enormous desk. His interior décor included Andrei Kushnir's *Potomac Riverscape* painting on the wall behind his desk. A Barbara Nuss oil painting of cherry blossoms hung facing his desk. Mr. Blackwell took pride in being an original Washingtonian. Framed photos of his wife and his parents were on his desk. A photo that caught Selma's attention showed him shaking hands with President Obama after a press conference. The photo hung right below the Potomac River painting.

Blackwell beckoned her to the seat in front of his desk. She glanced around the room and spotted a shot of Blackwell as a college student at Georgetown University with his lacrosse team. The long, wavy, dark brown hair he had during his college years was a sharp contrast from his current receding hairline.

"Thank you for taking time to see me, Mr. Blackwell," Selma said politely.

"You are welcome," he said. "And it is okay to address me as Steve."

"Thank you, Steve," Selma replied. Steve picked up one of the folders containing Selma's article and opened it. He flipped through the two pages and tapped his fingers on the desk gently. Selma could tell that he was not very impressed. She held her breath to avoid showing her uneasiness.

"For an audacious rookie journalist," Blackwell began, "I must admit that you did an excellent job showing how passionate you are about the issue of women in abusive relationships." Selma took a deep breath. It felt like an approval from a higher power.

"Thank you, sir," Selma said, swallowing the lump in her throat.

"I have to tell you, Selma. I have been curious about you as a black single mother and your background in journalism."

"When I sent my credentials to you, I sent copies of my undergraduate transcripts from the University of Lagos in Nigeria as well as my transcripts from Princeton," Selma said confidently.

"I am aware of that." Blackwell leaned back and continued. "I guess my concern is really the fact that English is not your first language and you speak with a slight African accent." He paused and took off his glasses. "It just makes me wonder how well you conduct your interviews. I'm just concerned, that's all."

His words stung like ten hornets. Selma dropped her head slightly and tried to conjure up the right words to say. She couldn't believe she was being stereotyped by her boss, but Selma remained poised, reminding herself that bigots were misguided, ignorant people with preconceived ideas about others.

Blackwell, a seemingly intelligent journalist, had a

worldview that was not as broad as she had thought; it fueled her determination to show him that she was good enough to be a successful journalist, despite his misconceptions of her cultural heritage. Selma's friends knew her well and would be surprised if she did not give Steve Blackwell a piece of her mind. She was not the kind of person to run from a fight. She knew then that she had to stand her ground and address the situation even if it meant confronting her boss.

"Well, Mr. Blackwell, when you read my article, was there any indication to you that I am not fluent in English?" Selma asked with a calm demeanor. "Were there some mechanical or structural errors that stood out to you?" Her sarcasm was deliberate.

"Selma, your piece is fine," Blackwell stammered. "There may be one or two editorial errors that can be easily fixed." He paused and continued. "You see, you are an African or African-American single mom, who works hard at what she does." Selma froze in her chair.

"With all due respect, Mr. Blackwell, I make no apologies for not fitting into your stereotype of the black single mother. And you're right; I work hard to be the best that I can be." Her voice fluttered. "I must say that I saw this coming, and I feel up to the challenge."

Blackwell leaned forward and adjusted his tie. "I admire your grit, Ms. Griffin. I am glad that you chose the *Uptown Gazette* to pursue your career in journalism."

"Thank you," Selma said and rose to leave. Impressed by Selma's resolve, Blackwell stood and held out his hand to shake Selma's. The tension between the two was obvious.

"Hey, good job on that Silver Spring shooting article," he said.

"Thank you, sir," Selma said and hurried out. She stopped at Jaden's cubicle, where he was typing an article about the scandal involving a congressman.

"Hi, Selma. The AP article gave us details about the corruption charges," said Jaden. "We're learning that this dude used some of the funds to buy expensive gifts for some female friends, if you know what I mean."

"I should get to work," Selma responded.

"Why don't you work on the house fire article?"

"Sure," Selma replied. "If I get some new information on Mr. Billingswood, I will send it to you."

"Sounds good," Jaden replied.

Selma hurried to her cubicle. She noticed four missed calls and a text from Christie. *Sorry about last night.* Selma rolled her eyes. *Logan is still in critical condition, and Afi went back to the hospital.*

Logan was a good guy and nothing like Selma's ex-husband or Martin. *Where is God in all this?* she thought.

Selma questioned her spiritually and the place of God in her life. The idea of good things happening to bad people, and bad things happening to good people like Logan, bothered her. Logan was in the hospital clinging to life, while Martin continued his reign of terror.

Selma did not notice Arianna outside her cubicle.

"Hi, Selma," she said.

"Oh, hi," Selma replied. She remembered that she should be working on the house fire article.

"Jaden wants me to ask you if you found any more information for him," Arianna said. "He wants me to have the draft ready for editing and the final draft ready for you guys to review before the end of the day."

"I'm on it," Selma replied.

She pulled up the Associated Press article about the shamed congressman and skimmed through it. The details were sketchy. She quickly opened a Word document and started typing her lead for the house fire article. Even though she hated to admit it, she knew that she worked better under stress. *The Hill Newspaper* had just posted an article about Charles Billingswood, citing a recent bill he co-authored about transparency among his fellow congressmen. Selma recalled a recent interview on *Meet the Press* where Congressman Billingswood made a statement that would haunt him. He explained to the moderator that every elected official had the moral obligation to account for every penny spent on anything. According to Mr. Billingswood, "Taxpayers who are footing the bill ought to know how their tax dollars are being spent."

Selma remembered the advice she had received from her ethical issues in journalism professor, Dr. Silverman. She had kept in touch with Dr. Silverman, and when she got the job offer at *Uptown Gazette,* she emailed him. Dr. Silverman's reply was curt: "Do not compromise your integrity by getting sucked into the whirlwind of mainstream news reporting."

Capital News Service was live-streaming news from the scene of the house fire in Montgomery Village Avenue and reporting that the fire had been contained, but the homeowners lost most of their belongings in the fire. Selma typed the news story, and included a quote by one of the neighbors who helped to save the lives of the elderly couple trapped in their house before it went up in flames. Arianna stuck her head in Selma's cubicle to inform her that Jaden had sent the article about the congressman. Selma stayed focused and completed the article and sent it to Arianna before opening her email to see article Jaden sent.

Although there was a big temptation to include salacious details about the congressman's extramarital affairs with three female college students, she decided to focus on accountability. It had been alleged he traveled overseas with young college students and bought expensive gifts for them, but Selma chose to talk about his responsibility to his constituents and the

American people. Arianna had Jaden's article on a split screen when Selma walked up to her.

"I just sent you mine," she told Arianna.

"I got it. Thank you. I will check on the house fire article as soon as I finish this."

Selma returned to her office and picked up her phone to return Christie's text. Two more texts had come in, one from Julie. Selma looked at her computer and noticed a newsfeed on the top of her screen. The Supreme Court had just ruled 6–3 in the pregnancy discrimination case of Young v. UPS. Selma remembered reading the article in the *Washington Post* on the Pregnancy Discrimination Act case and the treatment of a pregnant UPS worker who was forced to take unpaid leave instead of taking a position that was less strenuous for her. She made a note on a new word document stating, *Victory for Young in the Supreme Court case.*

Gary knocked on her cubicle and waited for Selma to respond.

"Hi, Gary," Selma said.

"A little birdie told me that we have a new columnist who can start work pronto," Gary said. Selma smiled.

"Thank you, Gary."

He pulled the chair in the corner closer to Selma's desk.

"I just finished my article about the indecision of Congress regarding immigration reform," Gary said. "If those guys would stop playing politics and solve this issue once and for all, it would help."

"I can't wait to read it," said Selma. "You know how to give attention to major issues."

"That's why I like satire," Gary said. "You cannot go wrong when you mix humor with serious business." After a short pause, Gary's countenance changed.

"I met a young man at the Bethesda YMCA last summer, his

name is Diego. He worked as a janitor. I saw him mopping the floor in the lobby with such diligence; you could see that he was doing his very best. I went back a month later, and Diego was gone. He had been deported because he was undocumented."

"That is so sad," Selma remarked. "You know I admire your courage and your wit, Gary."

"You are the first person to know that I pay people to read my articles," Gary said. "If you have to guts to read my article, the least I can do is to pay for your pain and suffering." Selma laughed.

"You are too funny," said Selma.

"Now to serious business," Gary said, clutching his hands to emphasize his point. "You want to make your column stand out, don't you?"

"What do you mean?" Selma asked. Gary leaned forward and placed both hands on the desk.

"A good journalist flows with the tide and writes what happens," said Gary. "A great journalist, however, rides the waves and writes stories that bring the experience to life."

"Now this is deep, Gary."

"My sister-in-law, Cecil, called my wife yesterday, and these two women talked for over an hour."

"About what?" Selma asked.

"She met some guy online and the two had been dating, if you call that dating," said Gary. "This guy turns out to be a big fraud." Selma had a puzzled look. "You don't seem to see where I am going with this."

"I am still not getting it."

"Two words," Gary said, holding up two fingers. "Online dating!"

"What can I say about it?" Selma asked. "Oh, I see."

Gary nodded and stood to leave. "If I were you, I'd do some investigative journalism on the issue."

"You mean going online and meeting people?" Selma asked.

"Writing about online dating using firsthand experience would make more sense to your readers," Gary said. "I imagine that they are scores of women out there who have had interesting experiences in internet dating, and some that have been duped." Gary held the door handle.

"That would be an interesting feat, Gary," Selma said, still not convinced.

"Just a suggestion, kid," said Gary as he walked out of the office. "I want you to stick around for a long time." He winked.

"Gary, you are a genius," Selma exclaimed. It could be the big break she needed.

NINE

A parcel in a big brown envelope was stuffed inside of Selma's mailbox. The package was soft and flexible. Selma carefully removed all the contents of her mailbox and headed into the house. The parcel had a London return address. She knew it was from her brother, CJ. The smell of basil and oregano overpowered the living room and kitchen. Kendra emerged from the kitchen wearing one oven mitt.

"Hi, Mom. I'm making pizza—homemade pizza."

Selma greeted her daughter and sank into the sofa. The day had been an emotional rollercoaster. After work, she had decided to go to the hospital to see Afi and Logan.

Selma placed the envelope from London on the dining table and opened it. A small card dropped on the floor. *Hey Sis, I hope you are doing well. I'm back from home. Mom says hi. You need to call her.* Selma smiled and removed a purple silk dress with gold thread embroidery. It had some beads around the neckline. Selma held up the dress and a transparent Ziploc bag containing a bracelet. Kendra emerged from the kitchen carrying a plate of pizza.

"Ashley's mom used flat Mediterranean bread to make individual pizzas," Kendra said as she sat in the chair across from her mother. "I decided to try, and it tastes good." She took a bite.

"It looks good," Selma said, admiring the intricate details of the silk dress she had removed from the bag. Kendra noticed the dress and jewelry.

"Who sent you those?"

"Uncle CJ," Selma responded. "Have you done your homework?"

"I've done my math homework, but I need to read two chapters in my English novel."

"I can't believe what I am going to ask you to help me do," Selma said.

"What is it?" Kendra asked with a mouthful.

"Create a dating profile for me," Selma said. Kendra's jaw dropped and her eyes lit up. "It is for work, Kendra." Selma rolled her eyes. "I know it sounds strange, but I mean it this time."

"Dating is part of your job?" Kendra was flabbergasted. "I thought you wrote newspaper articles. What has dating got to do with it?" Her eyes bulged.

"I will explain later," Selma said.

"What have you done with my mother?" Kendra joked. Selma smiled.

Kendra saw her as a typical Nigerian mother, who admonished her to wait until she was at least nineteen to date. Kendra had asked Selma why she was not in a relationship after the divorce. Selma did not want to admit her fear of another failed relationship.

Selma pushed the piled-up letters and the outfit to the edge of the dining table and went into the kitchen. As much as she looked forward to coming home after work and eating dinner with her daughter, their tastes differed. Selma enjoyed a Nigerian dinner of rice and tomato stew while Kendra would rather eat a sandwich, chicken nuggets, or pizza.

After eating, Selma took her bag and new outfit up to her room. The time difference meant that it was slightly past midnight in England.

"I've finished my homework, Mother," Kendra called from her room. "Are you ready to do your dating profile?" Selma smiled and shook her head.

"After I read your essay," Selma replied. Kendra conceded and let her read her essay about one of the characters in Harper Lee's *To Kill a Mockingbird.* Selma read Kendra's analysis of Scout Finch's character.

"Wow, Kendra! Your idea of Scout as a non-conformist is impressive!" Selma exclaimed. She pointed out two spelling errors and Kendra corrected them.

"You have it in you, Kendra. Excellent!"

"Thank you, Mother," Kendra replied. "Now, let me create the best dating profile known to mankind."

"This may be one huge adventure that I hope I don't live to regret," Selma said. Kendra closed her word document and logged onto the internet.

"Mom, don't be so petrified," said Kendra. "It's only a dating profile and people do it all the time." Selma sat next to Kendra on the bed and watched as Kendra did a Google search of internet dating. Over ten sites popped up on the first page. Selma cringed. She began to have second thoughts. She remembered what her father had told her about pursuing a career in journalism: "You must be ready to risk it all to gain it all." In a moment of epiphany, she realized that this could make or break her dreams.

"Mom, you need to do this," Kendra said. For those split seconds the roles were reversed. Selma sat back on the bed, watching Kendra.

"What in the world am I doing?" she stated. "This may not

be a good idea after all."

"Let's see here," Kendra said as she clicked on the *Ultimate Love Match* dating site. Selma was still hesitant. Kendra read the introduction on their homepage out loud.

"This seems like the right place for you, Mom" Kendra said. "It is safe, and you are guaranteed to find the right match."

"Yeah, right!" Selma exclaimed and rolled her eyes. "So, tell me, how do they know the right match?" She stood and walked around the room. "I am not too sure about this."

"Mom, it is the internet, you can be anything or anyone you want to be," Kendra said loudly. "Besides, you don't even need to use your real name." Selma cast a suspicious glance at Kendra.

"How do you know these things?" Selma inquired. "Have you done this before?"

"No, I do not have a profile, but one of my friends told me that she posted something."

"And?"

"I don't know, Mom," Kendra said, still focused on creating the profile. "Now, let's call you Lucylove39, looking for her forever Prince Charming." Kendra typed as she spoke.

"Why thirty-nine?" Selma asked.

"I want to pretend that you are thirty-nine years old," she replied, typing up Selma's profile as a registered nurse at Johns Hopkins. Selma laughed at the absurdity of it all.

"And what if some man decides to meet Lucylove39?" Selma asked. "Don't you already see the deceit in this type of practice?

"Well, she simply doesn't exist," said Kendra with a smirk.

"This is wrong on so many levels," Selma said. Kendra was quick to remind her of her job.

"Mom, think about this as working undercover to expose some terrible things about internet dating," Kendra said.

The doorbell buzzed.

"Don't post anything yet, Kendra," Selma cautioned.

"Mom, you need to relax," Kendra replied. "You can be anyone you want to be on the internet, don't forget that."

"I mean it," Selma said, wagging her finger. The doorbell buzzed again, and Selma rushed downstairs.

Habibah wiped her feet on the doormat and hugged Selma.

"Hi, Selma," Habibah said. "I hope this is not a bad time."

"You are always welcome here, Habibah," Selma said. "What can I get you?"

"Oh, don't worry yourself. I already ate dinner," Habibah said as she sat in the sofa. "Where is Kendra?"

"She's upstairs creating a dating profile for me," Selma said casually.

"Did I miss something?" Habibah asked. Her eyes were transfixed on Selma.

"It's for work," Selma explained. Habibah looked even more perplexed.

"What! Please tell me it has not come to this." Habibah clasped her hand together and raised her eyes toward the ceiling. Selma laughed. Kendra came downstairs and announced that she had completed the profile. The devious look on Kendra's face stunned Habibah, but Selma and Kendra thought it was hilarious.

"Why don't you bring the computer here," Selma said. Kendra sprinted upstairs and returned with the laptop a few minutes later. She read the profile out loud, and Habibah listened in awe.

"Please help me understand what is going on. *Please*," Habibah pleaded, still too surprised to laugh.

"I will be doing some investigative journalism," Selma explained.

"It is like going undercover to write about internet dating," Kendra added.

"I see where this is going," Habibah nodded. "One of my friends told me that she met someone online, and after three months of communicating with this man, they agreed to meet.

And then he asked her for transportation money."

"That person may not be real and could even be using a different name," Kendra said. Selma read the profile again and looked at Kendra.

"So this is a problem, and I will expose it," Selma said. "This begins my big dating adventure."

Kendra posted the profile on the *Ultimate Love Match* website. She patted her mother on the back and went back to her room. Habibah did not seem convinced, but she shrugged and leaned back in the sofa as Selma checked the website one more time before closing the laptop.

"How is Afi?" Selma asked. Habibah waited a few seconds before responding.

"I saw her this morning before I went to work, and they talked about hospitalizing her," Habibah replied.

"Christie called me earlier to inform me that Afi had been put on complete bed rest. She went to the hospital earlier, but did not stay too long because Afi was getting examined, and Logan was not allowed to have visitors."

"At least Logan will survive," Selma said.

"The question is how well he will be when he gets out," Habibah said. She did not feel like boring Selma with the neurological implication of Logan's situation. When she was getting her nursing degree, she worked briefly with a neurosurgeon and had a clear understanding of how Logan's brain could be permanently damaged. She rose to use the bathroom while Selma went into the kitchen. Selma returned with two containers of Greek yogurt.

"Was it Christie who told you about the shooting?" Habibah asked as she came out to the bathroom. Selma offered her one of the yogurts.

"Christie called me on the day of the shooting, and I went to the hospital with her," Selma said.

"She told me that you had a falling out with Martin," Habibah said.

"Did she tell you what she did?" Selma asked.

Habibah became uneasy. "She was unhappy about the way you left."

Selma finished the last bit of her yogurt and placed the empty container on the coffee table.

"I'm sorry, I don't need to take this out on you," Selma said.

"I understand," Habibah replied. "So, what really happened?"

"You saw us at Afi's home the night of the shooting, right?" Selma asked.

"Yes," Habibah replied.

"I had gone with Christie to visit Logan at the hospital. When we got to her house, Martin came out and berated me for being unmarried and gallivanting with Christie."

"Where was Christie?" Habibah asked.

"She stood there and said nothing while her husband ranted. She went into the house as soon as her coward husband ordered her, and she has not mentioned it since then."

"You know how much Christie is suffering at the hands of that bastard," Habibah said.

"That man is insecure, controlling, and deranged, if you ask me," Selma said.

"Martin is a bully and Christie is stuck between a rock and hard place," Habibah said. Selma had very little sympathy left for Christie. She shook her head and stared at Habibah.

"Martin has been bad news from the beginning, and over the years Christie has allowed him to treat her like a doormat."

"So you see, Christie is a victim, and we are her closest friends," Habibah said. "It is up to us to help and support her." She saw a more empathetic expression on Selma's face for the first time.

"You know, Habibah, a woman that has been a great inspiration to me once said, 'No one can make you feel inferior without your consent,'" Selma said.

"Selma, you need to understand where we come from," Habibah admonished. "Not everybody is bold enough to stand up for themselves." Selma nodded and had to concede that Christie's lack of confidence was a problem. She recalled how happy Christie had been the day she married Martin. Marriage gave her a sense of fulfillment.

Habibah's phone rang. It was her son. Selma pondered what Habibah had said and realized that Christie did need her. Although she could rationalize her disapproval of Christie's behavior, Christie was the one still stuck in a toxic marriage.

Habibah got off the phone and told Selma that she had to leave. Her son worked at the Subway restaurant in the mall and needed a ride home. Selma thanked Habibah for coming.

"I can't wait to hear about your dating adventures," Habibah joked as she picked up her purse to leave.

"I'm looking forward to that myself," Selma replied with a wink.

"I still have a hard time believing that you are putting yourself up to this," Habibah said.

As a non-devout Muslim woman, Habibah considered herself part of the demographic of educated and independent women who did not conform to the expectations of a typical Muslim wife. Her liberal views on religion allowed her to have very close friends like Selma, who was Christian.

"You know what they say: on the internet, you can be anyone you want to be," Selma said.

"If I ever decide to date online, I will present myself as Naomi Campbell or some Hollywood superstar," Habibah teased. "Then I will get plastic surgery." Selma chuckled. She hugged Habibah at the door and watched her walk to her car.

TEN

Selma had formed the habit of getting to the office early. Lisa was the only person there when she arrived Thursday morning. They exchanged glances, and Selma went into her office. Her first order of business was to pull up her column and do some final editing. The newsfeed indicated a slight growth in the US economy despite conflicting reports about the housing market. Selma focused on her article and edited the first page. Jaden hurried past her office without stopping.

A call came in from Habibah. Selma was surprised to learn that Afi had given birth at just thirty-six weeks. Afi started having severe contractions and had to be rushed to the hospital. Her baby boy arrived healthy, weighing just under six pounds. Selma was relieved and told Habibah she'd visit her friend after work.

Logan was still in critical condition. He had been stabilized but was very heavily sedated. Elaine Fisher, Logan's mother, was the only one allowed in the delivery room. Christie and Habibah had stayed in the waiting area.

The final draft of Selma's article was ready for publication. Jaden suggested a new title: *Staying Put Even When Love*

Hurts. Selma reread the article and felt a sense of pride and accomplishment. It was going to be in the Sunday issue, and it was time to start on the next column.

Her mind went to Afi, who would be raising a toddler at forty. It seemed like a no-brainer to write about women having babies later in life. She thought about celebrities like Halle Berry and Tina Fey, who had babies in their forties and remained symbols of elegance and beauty. Selma opened a document and started her lead paragraph before checking her email. Jaden had sent an email about ten minutes earlier alerting her to a developing story in the Associated Press about an attack on the consulate in Benghazi. She skimmed the article and learned that the ambassador and three other Americans had been killed in the blast. She went to Jaden's office and saw him frantically typing the breaking news.

"Scan the AP and UPI airways for details, and let me work on putting the article together," Jaden said without looking at Selma. It was a reality check Selma needed to understand the demands of her job. She enjoyed the thrill of observing history in the making and writing to inform the public.

A few more details emerged about the bombing. This had the makings of the kind of big story that journalists craved. As she skimmed the AP news report, another breaking report from Capital News Service scrolled across her screen. There was an accident on the beltway involving a big truck and several cars blocking the inner loop. Her instinct was to continue working on the big news event from overseas, but she instinctively knew that a local news story would be more relevant to *Gazette* readers. Jaden concurred that she should report on the accident. The AP and other wire services would provide details from Benghazi.

The hectic nature of this job began to sink in. She needed to be nimble and fast, and working at the *Gazette* would take all of her energy. She began to consider quitting her second job at Montgomery College. Although being an adjunct professor was part time, teaching a class in a community college served a bigger purpose for Selma. She thought about her students, Tyrone Wilson and Gladys Anderson in particular, and realized that she could be the inspiration they needed.

The challenges Gladys faced typified the challenges middle-aged women faced. As a single mother herself, she could empathize with Gladys's hardship. At the same time, she considered the vicious cycle of poverty that permeated families like Gladys's. The lack of proper education, raising a son without a positive role model, and having to raise a grandchild amid all the commotion were bigger problems that Selma wished she could solve.

"A penny for your thought, Ms. Griffin?" Gary said as he stood outside Selma's cubicle.

"Just the person I need to talk to," Selma replied.

"So, I hear your column is about to debut in the *Gazette*," Gary said, smiling broadly.

"It feels good to see your dream become a reality before your very eyes," Selma replied.

"You need to believe in yourself, kid," Gary said as he sat down. Selma could sense a close working relationship growing with Gary. "You are who you make yourself out to be in this business."

"I can never thank you enough for believing in me, Gary," Selma said, reaching out to hold his hand. "I'm sure you want to know about my internet dating escapade."

"Well, any fish in the net yet?" Gary asked raising his eyebrows.

"I haven't checked yet," said Selma. "I have a feeling this will be a wild ride."

"I knew from the outset that you, my friend, are a wild one," said Gary as he rose to leave. "On a serious note, this is solid investigative journalism."

"I will owe my success to you, Mr. Steinberg," Selma said. Gary smiled and gave her two thumbs up. Selma returned to her article. She recalled her father telling her not to be afraid to take chances. He would have been proud of her.

He worked as a head custodian at the Nigerian National Petroleum Cooperation (NNPC) in Port Harcourt for twenty-nine years before his death in late 1990. Selma wished he were alive to see how far she had come. She remembered his admonition about pursuing her dreams the day she graduated from the University of Lagos. "Stop fear in its tracks before it tries to stop you from fully attaining your dreams."

With renewed energy and inspiration, Selma worked on her article and almost lost track of time. She turned off her computer and packed up her bag to leave. A text came in from Kendra asking where she was. She responded, *Heading home and then to the hospital to see Afi and her baby. See you soon.*

Selma dragged herself into her living room and sank in the chair. She let herself imagine life with a child younger than Kendra, and what it would be like to be chasing a toddler around the house. Kendra was at the age where she could be left home alone. She knew how to heat up food and do some chores without being told. Selma was pleased that Kendra still maintained the routine she'd had since fourth grade. She ate a snack after school and did her homework before watching TV or going outside to play with her friends.

The house was quiet, and there was no sign of Kendra. Selma called, and when she did not get a response, she went up to Kendra's room. Her door was closed, but Selma could hear her talking on the phone.

"Kendra," Selma called.

"Mom, I'm in my room." She opened her door as Selma twisted the door handle. Kendra was on her cell. "I'm talking with Aunt Gertrude."

"That's nice," Selma replied. She knew her former sister-in-law was still on the phone and she didn't mind Kendra keeping in touch with her aunt.

"I'm sorry, Mom," Kendra said.

"Tell your aunt I said hi," Selma said.

She was not pleased that Gertrude was talking with Kendra because of the conflicting messages Kendra might get, yet she encouraged Kendra to have a relationship with her dad and his family. Selma went downstairs. She made a quick stop in the kitchen for a glass of water. Kendra sprinted downstairs and into the kitchen.

"Hey, Mom," Kendra said. Selma took a sip and placed the glass on the counter.

"Kendra, you need to be careful when you talk with your aunt," Selma cautioned. Kendra started to crack her knuckles, and Selma could sense that she was uneasy. "What's the matter?"

"She said Dad wants to see me."

Selma tightened her lips and glanced at Kendra. "What?"

"I did not mean to upset you, Mom," Kendra said. "You said you want me to relate to Dad's family."

"I'm sorry," Selma said, staring into her daughter's eyes. "I just don't want you to get hurt." She paused. "You just need to be careful."

"I will. I promise," Kendra replied. Selma hugged her.

"I love you," Selma said. "I have to go see my friend in the hospital."

"Mom, I can definitely take care of myself," Kendra replied.

Afi was sitting up in bed when Selma arrived. Four *Congratulations* helium balloons were next to the window and a bouquet of white roses in a pink jar was next to her bed. Mrs. Fisher, Logan's mother, sat next to Afi's bed. She beamed when she saw Selma and stood to greet her. The pain on Afi's face was obvious and there were dried tears under her eyes. In spite of her pain, she seemed fairly calm and poised. Selma placed a jar filled with mixed-color carnations on the counter and hugged Afi gently.

"Thank you so much for coming," Elaine Fisher said as she pushed the flower vase gently away from the edge of the counter.

"Congratulations on the birth of your grandson," Selma said. Elaine smiled and pulled another chair up to Afi's bed for Selma to sit on. Afi adjusted her blanket and used the button to adjust her incline. Elaine lowered the volume on the television.

"Where is the baby?" Selma asked.

"At the nursery ward, just as a precaution," Afi answered, sounding tired. Selma tried to conceal her sadness. Elaine stood and walked towards the door.

"He's a few weeks premature but healthy and cute as a button," Elaine said with pride. With the stress of the shooting and her son fighting for his life, Selma admired Elaine's resilient spirit. The smile on Elaine's face and the calm on Afi's were reassuring.

"Afi, is there anything I can do for you?" Selma asked. Afi shook her head and mouthed "pray." Selma held her hand and assured her that everything would be all right. Afi fought back tears. She tried to cough to clear her throat, but the pain from the surgery was intense. She placed her hand on her tummy and tried to cough again. Elaine brought a box of tissues to her.

"Would you like to see the baby?" Elaine asked Selma. "He is down the hall, and I don't mind taking you to see him.

"That would be nice," Selma replied. "How is Logan doing?" Elaine hesitated, and for the first time, Selma saw her vulnerable side.

"He is doing well," Elaine said. "I just wish he had been around for the birth of his son." Her eyes quickly filled.

"He is a fighter," Selma said. "He will be around to spend a long time with his son." Elaine nodded and smiled.

When Selma returned from the hospital, Kendra was sitting on the sofa with her laptop. An empty wrapper from Subway lay carelessly on the coffee table.

"Hi, Mom," Kendra said, engrossed in what she was typing.

"Hi, Kendra," Selma said as she set her bag on the floor next to the staircase. She sat beside Kendra and leaned towards her.

"How was your hospital visit?" Kendra asked.

"Thank you for asking. Afi and her baby are doing fine."

"I have done all my homework, and I'm letting you know because that's your next question."

"It's intriguing to know that my daughter reads my mind," Selma said. She rose and went into the kitchen. "I guess you had Subway for dinner."

"I don't like that Nigerian spicy soup," said Kendra.

"And that's exactly what I'm going to have," Selma said.

"So, have you checked your dating status yet?" Kendra asked in her unmistakably mischievous tone.

"I'm about to," Selma said, relishing the new phenomenon that had brought Kendra closer to her.

As a mother and daughter, their squabbles sometimes got out of control. It was always comforting to see the affectionate and contrite sides of her daughter. Kendra showed a great deal of maturity and sensitivity in the way she handled Selma's reaction to the phone conversation with her aunt. It was in sharp contrast to an earlier episode when Kendra had insisted on going back to Nigeria to stay with her dad. She had been ten years old then. Kendra scolded her mother and accused her of being responsible for breaking up their family. Selma worked hard to regain Kendra's trust, and their relationship improved.

Selma's heart raced as she turned on her computer. Kendra offered to help since she had thirty minutes before her bedtime. Curiosity and a sense of adventure intertwined as Selma watched Kendra open her page.

Kendra had edited an old passport photo of Selma and created a moving shadow image to obscure it. Kendra smiled and looked at her mother.

"What?" Selma asked.

"You have eight winks and six flirts," Kendra said.

"This is like a big joke," Selma said.

"Well, let's read the messages," Kendra rubbed her hands together and read them out loud. "Koolguy69 said, 'You are the woman of my dreams; the woman I have waited for all my life.' Jazzman said, 'Would you invite me to your heart?'" Selma laughed uncontrollably. "Mom, it gets better," Kendra continued. "Loverboy47 said, 'I want to meet you so bad it hurts; I am falling in love with you already,' and Devin001 said, 'I would like to get to know you. I have a feeling that you will complete me.'"

"So, I have to decide which of these to respond to, right?" Selma asked.

"You could respond to one or two of them," Kendra said. She was basking in her role as love coach for her mother. Jazzman's profile looked impressive. He was a forty-nine-year-old African American, and a father of two daughters, ages nine and twelve. He worked as a real estate agent and wanted a professional woman with strong Christian values. Part of Jazzman's profile read, *My philosophy is to treat people the same way I would like to be treated. Respect for human dignity is my number one principle. I am looking for a real woman who can complete me.*

Selma thought it sounded too good to be true. If anything, his profile raised more questions, and she decided to respond to him to satisfy her curiosity.

Devin001's profile was equally impressive. He was the owner of a European-style boutique and considered himself spiritual. Based on the photo on his profile, he was a Caucasian with very dark hair. *I am a conservative and financially secure man with many business interests and corporate entities in the US and in*

Europe. My ideal woman is a woman who is fashion conscious and neat in appearance. My interest is traveling, and I enjoy taking cruises around the world. I am successful businessman, ready to share my wealth with the right woman.

Selma sent Jazzman a short note letting to let him know that she was interested. She received a response from Jazzman, a.k.a. Ricky, in less than an hour.

Selma thought about the anonymity of internet dating and wondered how true the claims were. The idea of meeting random people and hoping to make a real connection seemed promising, especially with modern technology and social networking. However, the propensity for fraud made internet dating a dangerous game of chance. The realization that people were not exactly who they said they were when they created those profiles online was very unsettling. Selma had to put her idealism aside and face the reality of living in the computer age. Women like her had challenging jobs as well as families that demanded their attention; therefore, it made sense to turn to the internet. As far as Selma was concerned, the safety of this practice needed to be examined, and she hoped that her investigation would lead to discovery in some sense. She refused to entertain the thought of finding real romance through this means.

ELEVEN

The Sunday Edition of the *Uptown Gazette* hit Selma's doorstep, and she couldn't wait to read it. But first came church.

The Sunday morning sermon was unusually long. Reverend Jim Ballenger gave the congregation a chance to testify and give thanks for what God had done for them recently. For Selma, giving God thanks seemed like the appropriate thing to do on the first day of her column. She listened as parishioners gave touching testimonies about things they were thankful for. Selma clapped after the testimonies of an electrical engineer and a recent college graduate who had gotten a job at Lockheed Martin as an information systems analyst. Some of the testimonies were thinly-veiled bragging. That seemed especially true of Kent and Rosie Hilton, who gave thanks for an oceanfront home they had recently purchased in the Outer Banks of North Carolina. Kent took time to explain how important the home was to his family, and Rosie sobbed when she talked about how much it would help to get away from the daily stresses of life and find a peaceful oasis for reflection. The Hiltons invited parishioners to their home for a barbeque.

Selma took about three and a half minutes to give thanks for her column. She felt uneasy talking about her accomplishment, but applause erupted after her testimony. It's been about a month since she started working at the *Gazette*.

"Mom, I am very proud of you," Kendra said after the service. Selma smiled and patted her shoulder.

"I am glad it worked out," Selma said. "Now I need to call Grandma and Uncle CJ when we get home." Kendra gave her mom a fist bump.

That afternoon, Selma contemplated having a baby shower for Afi, and wondered if anyone else had planned one. She'd check with Christie.

Selma stretched out on the sofa focusing briefly on her toenails. The dark red nail polish was chipping off around the edges. She glanced at her fingernails and was satisfied that they still had a slight glow of the same red nail polish she'd worn for slightly over a week. She reached for her cell in the side pocket of her hand bag that was on the floor next to the sofa.

"I need to take off these church clothes," Kendra said and scampered upstairs to her room. She hurried back downstairs a few minutes later with her phone in her hand and feeling agitated. Selma told Habibah that she'd call back and hung up.

"You would not believe who just called," Kendra said, pacing from side to side.

"Who?" Selma asked.

Kendra covered the phone. "My father."

"Okay," Selma said, trying to find the right words to say. "Did he tell you why he called?" Selma needed to keep calm and not show the anger that she felt at that moment. It was her day to enjoy her success and look forward to a better life, and her ex-husband seemed determined to ruin that. Kendra sprinted back upstairs with the phone still in her hand. Selma rose and paced, trying to figure out what to say to her daughter or her ex-husband.

"He said he will call back to talk to you," Kendra said as she hurried back down to the living room. "He told me that he's been thinking of me." She went into the kitchen and returned with a bottle of water. Selma stood transfixed, still trying to figure out how to respond. "My dad sure has a strange way of showing his love."

"Okay, you need to remember," Selma said, "he is your father."

"He is not my father," Kendra snapped. Selma understood some of the pain and humiliation her daughter felt. Kendra had stopped asking where her dad was when a student at school taunted her for lying that her father worked for a cruise line and was away at sea. For as long as Kendra could remember, she had lied about her dad's whereabouts. Kendra rose and went upstairs to her room. Selma knew not to follow her.

Kendra's face lit up about an hour later when Selma walked into her room and asked her to check the *Ultimate Love Match* website with her. Kendra moved to give Selma room on the bed. "I know things are heating up with you and Devin001," Kendra teased.

"You should—Oh no, you should not see his recent emails," Selma chuckled.

"What have you been doing behind my back with some strange man, Mother?" Kendra asked. She smiled as she opened Selma's page. Kendra was quick to announce five more flirts and three winks. A text came to Kendra's phone.

"Mom, Latisha wants to know if I can go to the mall with her."

"Who is Latisha, and how are you going?" Selma asked.

"She's a new student in my biology class, and her dad will take us," Kendra answered.

"If he takes you, I'd be glad to bring you back," Selma said.

Kendra hugged Selma and thanked her.

"You know the rules, though; I need to meet this friend." It seemed like a prayer answered because Selma wanted some time to read her column and check on her infamous dating profile. Soon there was a knock on the front door.

"Well, you don't have to wait to meet Latisha," Kendra said as she hurried downstairs to open the door. Selma followed. A lanky teenage girl with big brown eyes and long braids walked in.

"Hello, ma'am," Latisha greeted.

"Hello," Selma replied. She noticed sparkles on her manicured nails. Latisha was wearing a pair of skinny jeans and oversized striped knit shirt.

"Mom, this is Latisha," Kendra said.

"Nice to meet you, Latisha," Selma replied. "Kendra said your dad is taking you to the mall, is that right?"

"Yes, ma'am," Latisha replied.

"Make sure you stay safe, okay?" Selma said. She glanced at the gray Toyota sedan parked next to her car.

"Bye, Mom," Kendra said and left with Latisha.

Selma immediately dove into her article. Her eyes filled with tears as she read the title and the byline in the column section of the *Gazette*. She wished her dad was alive to read it. She picked up her phone and called her mother. After two failed attempts, she gave up. With a deep sense of accomplishment, Selma decided to celebrate with a glass of sparkling apple cider, and took it up to her room. A line from Reverend Ballenger's sermon came to mind: "We need to realize that we live and work for a purpose greater than ourselves." She welcomed the thought that her article could help someone. She felt the pressure to work on her next article, and it meant following through with the dating-disasters article.

Skimming through emails on the dating website filled Selma with dread, but she maintained a journalistic mindset, hoping to expose fraud in online dating. There was another email from Ricky, a.k.a. Jazzman. Her mind went to the telephone conversations she'd had with him.

Ricky told her that he owned properties in five states, including a beach house in Florida. He invited Selma to visit him in Florida. The conversation seemed normal at first, even though Selma had no plans to visit Mr. Jazzman. The phone line had been fuzzy and his voice was not clear, but Selma gave him the benefit of doubt. Two days later, he called Selma and told her that he was in Mexico and had been robbed. He needed $650 to help him buy a ticket and fly back to the US because the thief had stolen his return ticket as well. Selma shook her head in disbelief. Jazzman went on to tell Selma that she was his only hope, and it was urgent because his safety was in jeopardy. She asked him if he had contacted the US embassy. He was ready with a ludicrous answer; he claimed he couldn't go to the embassy because the thieves had stolen all his decent outfits, and he did not look presentable. Selma found it revealing that he talked about his appearance and did not say anything about his passport.

In keeping up with the charade, Selma promised to call him when she found the money to send him. Minutes after hanging up the phone, she saw an email from Ricky, which read, *Hi sweetie, I feel very lucky and blessed to find someone who accepts and loves me for who I am. I just want you to know that I am totally committed to you and will never let you down. Your heart and your words speak to me.*

A recent email from Devin read, *Hello Beautiful, I woke this morning thinking about you. I hope you have a good day. I would like to see you soon. Please let me know where and when. Yours forever, D.*

Selma knew that she could continue to communicate with Ricky and Devin to get more materials for her article, but she had enough to start. Her experiences with Ricky and Devin already exposed the dishonesty of some people dating online, giving her a renewed mission to warn women who fell for these scams. Her mind went to the show *To Catch a Predator*, and she felt empowered to expose the bad guys.

A call came to her cell from a restricted number. Selma picked up her phone and hesitated at first, but decided to answer it.

"Hello, this is Eric."

Selma was silent. He asked her about her job. Selma nearly dropped her phone when he informed her that he was outside her house. She rushed to her front door and noticed a light brown Buick Enclave in the parking space next to her Subaru Forester. She paced her living room and decided to go out and confront him. She stood on the porch and shook her head in disbelief. Eric got out of the car and walked toward the house.

"What do you want?" Selma cried. "You have no business coming to my residence." Eric put both hands in his pockets and continued to walk toward Selma. He was wearing taupe double-pleated pants and a light brown batik-print shirt.

"How are you doing, Selma?" he asked arrogantly.

"You are not welcome here," Selma retorted.

"I came to see my daughter, if that is okay with you," Eric replied. "Where is she?" He stopped a few yards from the front steps. Selma moved away from the door and stood with one hand on the iron railing and the other arm akimbo.

"You really have some nerve, Eric Bawa," Selma said.

"I may not be anything to you, but you could at least let me see my daughter," he said softly.

"She is not here," said Selma. "After over seven years, I doubt that you know what she looks like." Eric turned to walk away, but changed his mind.

"Are you not inviting me in?"

"You must leave these premises now or I will call the police," Selma demanded. Eric took a step forward as if to dare her; then he turned aside as if to show off his designer outfit.

"You are still the same, Selma," Eric said with a sardonic smile. "How selfish can you be?" Selma did not move. She gave him a defiant look, and without speaking, dared him to come any closer. Eric walked back to his car and turned around.

"Go ahead, call the police." Selma started dialing as she walked back into the house. Eric stood by his car. Selma called Kendra and asked her what time they planned on being at the mall.

"Tell Latisha's dad to bring you girls back, if he doesn't mind."

Kendra was happy with the arrangement because she got to spend more time at the mall.

Officers Philip Wilson and Renee Goodman pulled into an empty space on the other side of Selma's car. Eric leaned on the trunk of his car waiting for the officers to approach him. He had his phone in his hand and seemed to be texting, unperturbed by the arrival of the police.

"What seems to be the problem?" Officer Wilson asked as he walked closer to Eric.

"Good evening, officer," Eric said and reached his hand to shake the officer's.

"So, what is going on?" Officer Wilson asked Eric.

"I came from out of town to see my daughter, and her mother wouldn't let me see her." The female officer radioed the main office alluding to their location and reporting that it was a domestic dispute.

"I take it that you do not live here, is that correct?" the officer asked.

"No, I don't," replied Eric. "I just came to see my daughter, and unfortunately her mother has brainwashed her and continues to keep her from me." Officer Wilson directed Officer Goodman to go inside and talk with Selma.

"This matter has to be decided in court," the officer told Eric. "It is the judge who decides the custody and visitation arrangements."

"We have been to court, and all she did was tell lies to ruin my reputation," Eric explained. The female officer and Selma stood on her porch. Selma explained how Eric just showed up seven years after moving back to Nigeria following their divorce. Officer Goodman suppressed a flash of anger when Selma told her that he had not called Kendra after being gone more than half of her life, until the day before.

"How did he find her number?" Officer Goodman asked Selma.

"I know my daughter talks with his sister," Selma replied. "She must have given him her number." She looked over to Eric and noticed him talking passionately to the other officer. Officer Goodman directed Selma to go back into the house while she joined her partner. Both officers directed Eric to leave.

"The only way you can see your daughter is to go back to court and get a visitation order," Officer Wilson said. "In the meantime, you cannot be here, and I advise you not to try to contact your daughter without a court order." The two officers got into their cruiser and waited for Eric to leave. He got into his car reluctantly and pulled out.

Selma was sitting on her porch when the gray Toyota parked next to her car. Kendra and Latisha came out and hugged each other. A tall dark man wearing a driving cap emerged from the car. Kendra and Latisha headed for the house with the man walking close behind them. Latisha's big brown eyes and chin were almost identical to her father's.

"Hi, Mom," Kendra said.

"Hello, ma'am," Latisha said.

"Welcome back," Selma replied.

"Hello," the man said in a husky voice, reaching out to shake

Selma's hand.

"Mom, this is Latisha's dad, Mr. Harris," said Kendra.

"Tony Harris. Pleased to meet you."

"Selma Griffin, and thanks for bringing the girls back, Mr. Harris," Selma said casually. "I couldn't pick them because I had a slight emergency."

"It's okay," said Tony. Kendra and Latisha went into the house. Tony stood at the bottom of the stairs and placed his hand on the railing.

"Kendra tells me that you just moved to this area," Selma said.

"We moved up here from Atlanta," Tony said. "I'm glad that Latisha found a good friend at school."

"Kendra seems to be enjoying her friendship with Latisha," Selma said.

"Latisha told me that you are a journalist," Tony said, looking uneasy.

"I work at the *Uptown Gazette*," Selma said. "So where do you work, Tony?"

"I work at Walter Reed Army Medical Center as an anesthesiologist," Tony replied. Latisha and Kendra came out, each holding a granola bar.

"It's really nice meeting you," said Selma. "Thanks again for bringing Kendra back."

"It's my pleasure. Nice meeting you too," Tony said.

TWELVE

Waking up on Saturday mornings for class was beginning to take its toll. Selma decided that it was best for her to focus on the *Uptown Gazette*. Gladys's jaw dropped when Selma informed her class that it was going to be her last semester teaching at Montgomery College.

"I was hoping to take another class with you, professor," Gladys said. Selma tied her announcement to their discussion of Robert Frost's poem, "The Road Not Taken." During the discussion about the metaphor of the two roads, Selma encouraged them to connect the theme of the poem to their own lives. To Selma's surprise Tyrone Wilson raised his hand. The class was silent as he explained that the road not taken by people like him was being in school. He recited the last line to stress his point: "And that made all the difference." The class erupted in applause. Selma beamed with pride. On a few occasions, she had admonished Tyrone about his absences and told him not to give up on his music career. Tyrone agreed that getting a degree would broaden his chances to succeed in life.

A few minutes before the end of class, Selma opened the *Gazette* to her page and connected it to the poem. With her eyes fixed on Tyrone, she explained how staying in school and pursuing goals could provide opportunities. She hoped that they understood her reason for choosing to discontinue her job with the college. She concluded that writing her column was a road less traveled, and it made a real difference for her. The class cheered.

Selma made the eight-minute drive to Julie's home on Wootton Parkway. She had called earlier to make sure she was home. Kendra was babysitting MJ, and there was no reason to hurry home. Julie's car was not in her usual parking space. Selma pulled into the space and called from there to find out where she was. Julie stepped out of the second floor sliding door and beckoned Selma to come in.

"Where is your car?" Selma asked as she walked into Julie's condo.

"A friend has it," she replied. Selma cast a glance at her. It was quite unusual for Julie to let anyone else drive her Audi convertible. She called it her baby. Selma had not seen Julie in about a week because of work. She had to hurry home the previous week to work on her articles and to make time to visit Afi.

"This must be a very special friend," Selma said, sitting in the leather sofa and looking around the room. Julie grinned and gave Selma a mischievous look. Julie brought a bottle of water and a glass for Selma.

"Okay, spill the beans," Selma said as she poured the water in the glass. She noticed a hint of a blush on Julie's cheeks as she took a sip. It was clear that Julie was hiding something.

"I am seeing someone," Julie blurted. Selma swallowed the sip and let her jaw drop. She managed to get out one word.

"Congratulations!"

Julie sat in the recliner across from Selma.

"You know I have a lot of questions," said Selma. "First, how did you meet?"

"I will make it easy for you, Selma," Julie said in her usual brusque manner. "His name is Roberto. He's Latino, and he works as a computer analyst for National Institute of Standards and Technology."

"You mean NIST in Gaithersburg?"

Julie nodded. "I'm beginning to like this fellow," Selma said. She leaned back in the sofa, and Julie went into the kitchen. Alicia Keys's "This Girl is on Fire" was playing on the radio. Julie's Siberian cat, Boxer, sauntered into the living room and hopped onto the recliner. Selma rose and went to the patio. One more potted plant had been added to Julie's collection. The picturesque pond on the grounds of the congressional golf course was a short distance away.

Julie placed a plate of chicken quesadillas and a bowl of corn salad on the dining table. The aroma of cumin and cilantro filled the air. One of the things that Selma found fascinating about Julie was her love for cooking, because she could not imagine a busy woman like Julie finding time to cook and prepare for her cases. Selma went to the table and took some grapes from the basket. Julie stood at the window overlooking the parking lot and looked around.

"He's here," she announced.

"Who is here?" Selma asked, holding a grape in her mouth.

"Robby," Julie said.

"Robby. Is that what you call him?" Selma teased, putting another grape in her mouth. Julie opened the door, and a tall Hispanic man walked in holding a brown shopping bag from the local Latino grocery store. He bent over and kissed Julie on the cheek. Selma walked back to the sofa and sat next to Boxer, who had moved from the recliner to the sofa. Roberto was wearing gray sweatpants with the Maryland logo and a red, long-sleeved Maryland varsity shirt. His dark, unshaved beard added a couple of years to his real age, but he definitely looked like a man in his thirties, probably early thirties.

"Robby, I want you to meet my very good friend, Selma," Julie said.

"Hello, Selma. I've heard a lot about you," Roberto said in a deep baritone. He had a firm handshake. Julie smiled. Roberto went into the bedroom. Julie invited Selma to the dining table for brunch. She opened the refrigerator and brought a pitcher of lemonade.

"He is young," Selma whispered.

"Thirty-two," Julie smirked. She shrugged and glanced at the bedroom door before whispering, "He is very good to me."

"Well, I see that you are happy, and I'm happy for you," Selma said. Roberto joined Julie and Selma. He sat at the end of the table while Selma sat across from Julie.

"Julie told me you are a journalist," Roberto said with a noticeable accent.

"Yes, I just started working at the *Uptown Gazette*," Selma replied.

"It must be very exciting to work in the news industry," said Roberto.

"I like it a lot," Selma replied. Julie poured herself some lemonade and poured some for Selma and Roberto.

The conversation during the meal was congenial. Roberto refilled Julie's plate with the salsa while he indulged in the quesadillas.

"I love Julie's quesadillas," Roberto remarked. "They remind me of my mom's." Julie beamed. Selma cast a glance at him and then at Julie. They seemed happy. Roberto ate the last bite of the quesadillas and gulped down what was left of his lemonade.

"How is Afi?" Julie asked Selma.

"She is doing very well, and so is her husband," Selma replied.

"It was really nice meeting you, Selma," Roberto said as he rose from the table. He gathered the plates and took them into the kitchen.

"Thanks," Julie said to Roberto.

"Remember the festival is in two hours," Roberto said, and he put the dishes in the dishwasher.

"We can leave in an hour," Julie said to Roberto.

"Are you guys going somewhere?" Selma asked.

"There is a Latin folk festival at the National Mall, and we plan to attend it," Julie explained.

"You both seem so in love," Selma whispered. Julie smiled.

"I guess I am in love," she replied.

"I should be heading home," Selma said.

"How is Afi's baby doing?" Julie asked

"He is doing very well," Selma replied.

"That family has endured so much in a short amount of time," Julie said.

"I am thinking about throwing her a baby shower," Selma said.

"I think it will be a good idea," Julie said. "Is Christie going to help you?"

"I don't know," said Selma. "I'll have to ask her." Julie had made a conscious effort to stay out of the conflict between the two friends. Although Selma and Christie remained cordial, the tension between them was noticeable.

"Let me know what I can do," said Julie.

"Hey, would you bring some quesadillas to the party?" Selma asked.

"I'd be glad to bring some," Julie said.

Not very many people got to see the kind, helpful and considerate side of Julie. Even though her high energy and no-nonsense attitude in court could be intimidating, Julie was friendly and dependable. Selma was surprised that she was dating a man ten years younger, but it did not come as a shock. Julie's first advice to Selma was to make sure she defined herself and not let her circumstances define her.

Habibah opened the door at Christie's home when Selma arrived to pick up Kendra. That was a little odd. Selma could hear the sound of a video game from the basement and MJ cheering. Christie sat on the sofa hugging a pillow. Habibah sat next to Christie and beckoned Selma to sit on the other side. Selma glanced at Habibah and then at Christie before sitting.

Selma noticed the big bruise under Christie's left arm, and her initial anger turned into sympathy for her friend. She did not need anyone to confirm that Martin had beaten her again. Christie also had a slight bump just about her right eyebrow. The brown powder foundation did very little to conceal it.

"Another fight with Martin?" Selma asked. Christie nodded.

"This time he has decided to leave her," Habibah added.

"What?" Selma asked.

"Martin has left Christie," Habibah stressed.

"I am sorry that you are going through this," Selma said.

"Selma, I am sorry about our disagreement," Christie said. "You were right about Martin." Christie began to sob.

"I am here for you, Christie," Selma said and paused. "You have a long rough road ahead." MJ ran up from the basement with Kendra close behind. They ran into the kitchen and each got a Capri Sun pouch. Kendra noticed her mother just before she got to the stairs.

"I didn't hear you come in, Mom," Kendra said.

"We should be leaving soon," said Selma. "I'll let you know." Kendra and MJ ran back to the basement. Habibah went to the kitchen and brought back three bottles of water. Selma patted Christie's back, trying to process the next steps.

"In all honesty, Christie, you need all the support you can get," Habibah said.

"I will talk to Julie about it and see what she says," Selma promised. "Have you called your family in Nigeria to let them know what is going on with you and Martin?"

Christie shook her head. "You know how it is," she sobbed. "I need them to think that we are doing well."

Selma knew too well about family expectations. She recalled how her childhood friend in Nigeria, Ijima, called her a disgrace for being too "Americanized" and too ambitious for divorcing Eric.

"The problem we have is that our society and our culture expect us to pretend that we are living in paradise even when we are living in hell," Habibah said. "Our parents believe that it is our job as women to keep families no matter what."

"And that is why we care so much about presenting our perfect families to our friends and relatives so that they don't judge us," Selma added. "But there comes a time when we have to stand up for ourselves."

"Aren't we supposed to be the good wives that we were raised to be?" Christie said. "That is why I try and ignore some of the things he does. MJ needs his father."

"When you got married, you did not sign up to be treated like a slave, did you?" Habibah said. "Your parents are alive, and they don't know what you are going through." Selma glanced at Christie. "I know they don't want to see you suffer." Habibah fought back tears.

"I will call my parents tomorrow," said Christie.

"You need to call and let them know what is going on," Habibah said shaking her head. "I wish I had my own parents."

"You know what?" Selma said, changing the subject. "I am thinking about having a baby shower for Afi." Christie's eyes lit up.

"You know I had planned to do it a week before the birth of her son," Christie said.

"This is good for Afi, and it will take our minds off the bad stuff." Selma suggested that they have a surprise party at Selma's house.

"Julie plans to be there as well," Selma said, hoping that Christie would make the connection.

THIRTEEN

Selma's first order of business at the *Gazette* was to start the lead for her article on internet dating after age forty. It had taken her two weeks to write her first column, and her goal was to finish the second column by the end of her fourth week at *Gazette*. She had two days to achieve that goal.

Online dating has become a lucrative and very daring venture for people of all ages, she wrote. She considered three possible headlines, but her focus was to write a lead and build on it. Engrossed in her article, Selma did not notice Steve Blackwell outside her cubicle.

"Hello, Ms. Griffin," Blackwell said.

"Oh, hi, Mr. Blackwell," Selma replied.

"Mind if I come in?"

Selma moved closer to her desk, pushing her keyboard aside.

"Not at all," she said. "I really appreciate you stopping by." Blackwell noticed her uneasiness as he sat in front of her. It was not unusual for the boss to stop by her office, but her first meeting with Blackwell made her realize that he did not have faith in her.

"I want to personally applaud you for your work at the *Gazette*, and especially for your sensational column," Blackwell said. He could tell that Selma was flabbergasted. She forced a smile as she flashed back to her first meeting with him.

"Coming from you that means the world to me," she said. Although she hoped that Blackwell's visit meant that he had renounced his stereotype of black women, she could not rule out a more sinister reason for his visit.

"Your column is not only getting the attention that we hoped for, it is setting you apart as a journalist to watch," he said. Selma felt pure exhilaration, and the moment had come a lot sooner than she expected. "By the way, Lisa and Arianna will be creating a weblog to help us manage the responses that we are getting about your column." He smiled and gave a thumbs-up.

"I guess that means I have a blog now?" Selma said.

"Indeed," Blackwell smiled as he walked out of Selma's office.

She paused to absorb the news. The realization that her column was creating a platform for her to interact with readers seemed like a crazy afternoon dream. She decided to continue working on her internet-dating article for her column. It was her first assignment as an investigative journalist, and Selma was ready to pour in her heart and soul to create an article she considered relevant.

Selma checked her email to see what she and Jaden were supposed to be writing. She noticed two congratulatory notes from Cynthia and Gary. Jaden's email was short and did not mention the article. He informed Selma that he had started working on a story about extreme athlete Felix Baumgartner after his historic space jump, and he needed her to check the Associated Press or any other wire service for stats about him. He seemed to be needlessly asserting his position as an assistant editor when he instructed Selma to do thorough research on Felix's time with the Austrian military and the places where he had trained and parachuted. Selma was a bit stunned by the condescending tone of his email and decided to talk to him directly.

"Do you have the stats on Felix Baumgartner?" Jaden asked Selma disdainfully when he saw her walking towards his office. Selma noticed him frantically typing and reading from a small notepad. A part of her considered that the pressure of work might have put him a bit over the edge, but she found it odd that all the emails she received from her colleagues were congratulatory, but his was more of a work order.

"Mr. Smith, I would appreciate it if you refrain from using that tone with me." It was the first time Selma addressed him by his last name.

"Well, Ms. Big Shot Celebrity-in-Training," Jaden mocked, "why don't you go back to your cubicle and do the job you are assigned."

Selma was visibly shocked by the remark, but she did not have reason to believe that Jaden had a nefarious intention. His behavior was uncharacteristic, and Selma decided that the pressure of writing and meeting a deadline could have set him off, even though there was also the possibility of jealousy.

"What is the matter with you?" Selma huffed. "Can you not stand the success of another person?" She was careful not to make it a feminist issue. Jaden continued typing and did not respond. Selma shook her head in disgust and walked back to her cubicle.

Selma emailed Jaden the information he needed, including Baumgartner's 2007 jump from the deck of the ninety-first floor of the tallest building in Taipei, Taiwan. She had considered Jaden a good colleague who had her best interest at heart. His strange behavior added to the unexplainable events that day. She leaned back in her chair and played back events that were both fascinating and scary. Eric showing up unexpectedly topped the list. Christie's impending divorce did not surprise Selma, but it was notable nonetheless. Julie had always been unpredictable, and it was not surprising that she would be dating a man ten years younger.

Another email from Jaden informed her that the article was complete. She closed her inbox and continued with her internet-dating column.

Her interaction with Ricky had the most profound effect on her. After his elaborate story about being a successful real estate agent, his story about being robbed in Mexico and needing money raised an obvious red flag that she hoped other women could learn from. At the same time, it was easy to understand how someone gullible and full of hope could believe his story and actually send him the money he was asking for.

Unscrupulous men in the dating world would lure you in with enticing words, and then go fishing for your hard-earned money, Selma wrote. She added a few quotations from her emails from Devin and Ricky. She had continued the charade to get the two men to give her more material for her article.

A breaking news story from the Associated Press streamed across Selma's computer and caught her attention. A bombing in Baghdad had killed over a hundred people and injured hundreds more. She paused to read the story. Once again, she suspended writing her article to focus on the breaking news. Selma was adjusting well to the spontaneity of the news world. Graphic images were beginning to emerge from the evolving story. Selma opened a document and wrote a lead. She started with the title *Scores Killed in Bagdad and Many More Injured.* She emailed the title and the lead to Jaden. She got a response less than five minutes later: "I'm on it." Selma walked over to Jaden's office. Jaden did not say anything.

"Would you like me to continue writing and send you what I have so you can merge them?"

"I told you, *I'm* working on the article," Jaden replied.

"Do I need to do some research and gather more information?" Selma asked.

"Why don't you focus on your article and let me write this?" Jaden griped.

"Fine," replied Selma. Clearly something was amiss, and she was making speculations that may not be true.

Selma left the office with a sense of accomplishment. Jaden was pulling out of the parking lot when she got to her car. She waited for him to leave. She always thought of him as a young African-American man who carried himself well. She recalled a conversation with Edna after church two weeks earlier. Edna agreed with Selma's views about women staying in abusive relationships because of fear. Edna looked in her eyes and told her that sometimes women acted out of fear, but men acted out of insecurity. Her mind went to Jaden, who was clearly competitive and a workaholic. He seldom talked about his family, friends or even a girlfriend.

A text came in from Habibah asking her to Christie's house. She wondered what time Habibah left her work to already be at Christie's. Working in a doctor's office had obviously given Habibah more flexibility. Habibah did not have the same understanding when she worked at NIH. Although Selma had not met Dr. Anita Freeman, she could tell that her friend's boss was very considerate.

Selma called to check on Kendra who had been spending most of her time after school with her new friend, Latisha. Just as Selma expected, Latisha was coming over to her house.

Selma noticed Habibah's car in the driveway when she arrived at Christie's house. Nothing seemed out of the ordinary when Selma went into Christie's house except that Martin's golf clubs were missing from beside the fireplace. All family portraits were still in their places. Christie looked despondent as she sat on the sofa holding a big brown envelope. MJ was sitting on the elevated base of the fireplace playing with action figure Lego pieces.

"Hi," Selma said to Christie as she sat next to her.

"Hi, Selma, thank you for coming," Christie said. Habibah emerged from the bathroom and joined Selma and Christie in the living room.

"Selma, sorry to drag you here after work," Habibah said as she sat on Christie's other side. Selma smiled and held Christie's hand as a sign of solidarity.

"That's what friends are for," Selma said.

"Can I get us something to drink?" Habibah asked. Christie and Selma shook their heads. Besides the ticking of the Bulova Norwood pendulum clock in the family room, the only sound in the house came from MJ humming the *Bob the Builder* theme song.

"So, what is the latest?" Selma asked.

"Martin just served me with divorce papers," Christie said, fighting back tears. "I need a lawyer." Selma's head dropped. Habibah patted Christie's shoulder. Nobody spoke for almost a minute. To Selma, this empty house decked with exotic paintings and photographs of family treasures felt like a lifeless seashell. She wished she could find a way to let Christie know that she could move on and find happiness elsewhere. It was time to get Julie fully involved.

"I'll ask Julie to give you a call," Selma said. Christie looked relieved. Even though she had known Julie for a short time, she felt an instant connection.

"I told Christie that her friends will be here for her," Habibah said. "Divorce is tough, and no one knows about this better than you, Selma."

"We are here for, Christie," Selma said. "If anyone can handle this, I know Julie can." Habibah nodded.

"Anyone who could put Eric Bawa in his place can definitely teach Martin the meaning of respect," Habibah remarked.

"Give me a little information for Julie," Selma said. "She would need to have something to help her plan before your first meeting."

"Well, Martin is seeking the divorce, and he wants to keep the house, our son, and our cars," Christie said. Selma laughed in derision, and Habibah joined in.

"I'm sorry, Christie," Selma said. "I hope you know I am not being insensitive. It's just too familiar."

"I understand," Christie responded. Selma leaned closer.

"You can rise up and take charge of this situation, or let it define you," Selma said firmly. "I can understand your fear, but you are about to find out just how strong you really are by facing your challenges head on."

Christie nodded. Two tear drops cascaded downward. Her pain was unmistakable. Despite her disappointment in Christie for not seeing all the red flags with Martin, Selma understood how much Christie needed her.

"Okay, now that we have a divorce attorney, let's plan a baby shower," Habibah said.

"We could have the party here at my house this weekend, right?" Christie asked.

"We could, but we need to figure out what each of us is doing," Habibah said. She looked through her purse and found a notebook. Habibah was known for her meticulous planning and for taking charge.

"Works for all," Selma replied. She had always admired Habibah's loyalty and dedication to her friends. She got to know her better shortly after her own divorce. Habibah had visited Selma often and made sure that she had food in the house and planned adequately for Kendra.

"Thanks so much for letting me host the party," Christie said to Selma.

"It is good thing for you to do this, and I know it would mean a lot to Afi," Selma said. "Julie will bring some Mexican food." Habibah wrote it in her notebook. Since she had been the last person to visit Afi at home, she had a few ideas for the shower presents that would be useful to her.

"This will be really good for that family," Habibah said. "Logan's recovery is nothing short of a miracle."

Logan had started his rehabilitation at the Adventist Center two days earlier. It was hard to imagine that Logan was talking and walking after a gunshot wound to the head. In spite of his slurred speech, Logan continued to be his jovial self.

"This baby shower couldn't have come at better time," echoed Selma.

MJ came into the living room and climbed on his mother's lap. He got up, gave her a gentle hug, and held her face with both hands.

"Are you okay, Mama?" he asked.

"I am fine, MJ," she replied.

"What's for dinner?" he asked. Habibah and Selma laughed.

"You *are* fine, now it's time to fix dinner," Habibah joked. Selma stood up to leave.

"I should be leaving now," Selma said. "Kendra will be asking for dinner too." Habibah decided to leave as well.

"Christie, if you need anything, please let us know," Habibah said. Christie smiled.

"Sometimes I wonder why I deserve friends like you guys," Christie said. She stood and walked Selma and Habibah to the door. She gave each a hug and thanked them for coming.

Habibah called Selma on her cell after they pulled out of Christie's cul-de-sac.

"It was short notice, but I really appreciate you coming," Habibah said.

"Christie is going to need us, and I believe it is the best we can do for a friend," Selma replied.

As Selma drove home, she pondered Christie's efforts to stay married to Martin. Shortly before the fallout with Martin, Christie had informed her that Martin's "friend," Geraldine Henshaw, recently got a job with the Nigerian embassy and worked at the consulate in New York. At forty-two, she was still unmarried. Selma could have predicted a divorce in Christie's future because she predicted that Martin was going to leave Christie for Geraldine. Selma did a Google search and found a photo on her Facebook page. Her image was that of a sophisticated, full-figured woman in her forties wearing diamond loop earrings and a matching bracelet. She flaunted a black leather Valentino handbag in her pose. Selma was sure it was the right Geraldine because she used the Nigerian flag as her backdrop. When Martin left, he drove his Cadillac Escalade to New York. Selma thought about the irony of Martin choosing Gerry over Christie as a clear sign of insecurity. She did consider that a plausible reason could be Geraldine's success in her career.

FOURTEEN

Colorful foliage, cool breezes and Thanksgiving were some of Selma's favorite things about the fall. With the holiday just a couple weeks away, Selma reflected on her family and friends, and the three columns she had written so far. She appreciated her daughter, her career, her friends, and her family in Nigeria. Her parents were in their late sixties and still healthy enough to tend to their farms. She found herself playing the role of big sister and protector to her friends.

As shc thought about Christie's impending divorce, it bothered her that she could not protect Christie from the pains of loneliness and feeling of failure that came with it. She decided to plan a low-key Thanksgiving dinner, and invited Habibah and her son. Christie was planning to travel to Florida with MJ to visit her uncle. It seemed like a good idea to plan Afi's baby shower for the week after Thanksgiving.

Selma made her signature jerk chicken with lime sauce for Thanksgiving with Kendra. Afi enjoyed Thanksgiving with her extended family, including Mawusi, Afi's mother, who was visiting from Ghana. Selma declined the invitation to Afi's home for Thanksgiving, but she invited Afi's whole family to a Sunday brunch.

Selma rushed home after church to cook bean cakes made from blended black-eyed peas. She made fried rice and white rice with beef stew. Habibah brought homemade ginger and lime juice.

Elaine and Mawusi seemed happy to go on their first family outing with their grandson, Max. Mawusi wore a four-piece green lace outfit with head gear, an elegant turquoise stone necklace, and earrings to complement her outfit. Elaine wore a two-piece African brocade dress that Mawusi brought for her.

"What a beautiful family," Selma exclaimed as she opened the door for the Fisher family.

"It was our first day at church," Afi said as she carefully placed the baby carrier on the floor next to the sofa. Her elegant blouse and burgundy, gold-plated lace skirt with rhinestones caught Selma's attention.

"Your outfit is beautiful," Selma said as she hugged her.

"My mother brought it for me," Afi said.

"Thank you, Auntie," Habibah said to Mawusi.

"Mawusi is responsible for our elegant looks today," Elaine said. Mawusi grinned. She placed a Kente tote bag on the floor next to her. Logan did not dress up like the rest of his family. In spite of his slurred speech and slightly disfigured face, Logan was cheerful and continually referred to himself as "one lucky Texan." He wore his Chris Cooley jersey proudly, and talked about being a Redskins fan from the Cowboy nation.

"We sent those Cowboys packing on Thursday," Logan said, struggling to speak clearly.

"Hail to the Redskins," Kendra added and gave Logan a high-five. Selma saw how happy Afi was and thought about the unique circumstances that brought Logan into her life. Max had a full head of hair. Even at four and a half weeks old it was easy to see how much he resembled Logan. Kendra sat next to Afi as she fed the baby. She offered to help.

"He is very cute," Kendra said. "Can I hold him?"

Afi held the baby close to her chest.

"Maybe when he gets a little older," she said lovingly. Logan could hardly keep his eyes off Max. Kendra stroked the baby's cheeks gently. Selma and Habibah went to the kitchen to finish cooking, while Kendra took out dinner plates and cutlery and placed them on the dining table. Logan bit into one of the bean cakes and asked Selma what she put in it. Selma smiled and promised to teach Afi how to make it.

"Why don't you give her the recipe?" Elaine asked. Habibah laughed.

"I don't use recipes when I cook," Selma replied. Elaine's eyes widened.

"We learn to cook by watching," Afi added. Logan ate all the fried rice Afi dished out for him and went back for seconds. Elaine took a sip of the ginger drink that Habibah brought.

"I guess asking for this recipe is also out of the question," Elaine said. "I would like to watch you make it, Habibah."

"I'd love to teach you how," Habibah replied.

"Selma, thank you for having us over for brunch," Logan said when they stood to leave two hours later. "You are a real friend. Afi is lucky to have you."

Mawusi opened her tote bag and gave Selma, Kendra and Habibah each a two-piece African brocade caftan. Inviting Afi to her home was befitting for a family that inspired her so much. The Fishers were everything she wished for in a family.

"Mom, Latisha wants to know if she can come over," Kendra shouted from her room.

"After we clean up and put the dishes away," Selma said. She knew that Latisha's visit was the incentive Kendra needed to help with the dishes without a fuss.

Selma had not given a thought to Latisha and Tony until then. Tony walked Latisha to the door when he brought her to Selma's house. He wore a pair of black sweatpants and a T-shirt. Latisha greeted Selma and joined Kendra, who was finishing up the dishes in the kitchen.

"Hello, Selma," Tony said. "Those two seem inseparable." Within the short time that Selma had known Tony, she got the impression that Tony was a hands-on dad. She was curious about Latisha's mom and about why she hadn't seen her or heard about her. Other questions about Tony swirled around her head. The noticeable strands of gray hair in his short beard made him seem like a guy in his forties.

"I'm glad that Kendra has a good friend," said Selma. "Would you like to come in for a minute?"

Tony answered with a questioning grin.

"I would like that," he said. He wiped his feet on the doormat and walked in. Kendra and Latisha could be heard giggling and carrying on in Kendra's room. He sat in the chair and moved closer to the edge. Selma sat on the sofa across from him.

"Can I get you anything?"

"No thank you," Tony replied. "I'm heading to the gym."

"You must work out a lot," Selma said, feeling awkward, but she couldn't think of something else to say.

"It's part of my military life, I guess," Tony replied. "I try to keep in shape." Selma smiled sheepishly, and leaned back on the sofa.

"I'm sorry for asking this, but I am curious to know." He paused for a few seconds to gather his thoughts. "Does Kendra's dad live here?" Selma cast a menacing look at him.

"No, he doesn't," she said sharply. Tony bit his lower lip.

"I'm sorry." Tony leaned back. "That was very presumptuous of me." They exchanged glances and smiled. Tony readjusted his sitting position and raised his eyes to the ceiling and looked around the house. Their daughters chattered upstairs. Less than a minute later, they scampered downstairs talking loudly about Taylor Swift's VMA award.

"Dad, I didn't know you were still here," Latisha said.

"Kendra's mom and I were just hanging out before I head to the gym," Tony replied.

"What have you girls been up to?" Selma asked.

"We are redecorating my room," Kendra said.

"Hey, if you are free, you could go to the gym with me, as my guest," Tony said to Selma.

"I would like that," Selma replied. Kendra glanced at her mother and then at Tony.

"What?" Selma asked Kendra.

"Nothing, just wondering," Kendra said. She and Latisha went into the kitchen and Tony rose to leave.

"Let me get dressed for the gym," Selma said. "It shouldn't take too long; I just need to throw on something comfortable.

"Not a problem," Tony replied. He took the liberty of walking around the room studying some of Selma's paintings. The one that got his attention was Thomas Kinkade's *Peaceful Retreat* above the sofa. Selma trotted downstairs in pink-and-black Capris and an oversized Maryland T-shirt.

"Ready?" Tony asked.

"A soon as I put on my sneakers." Selma replied.

After an hour of kickboxing aerobics and a thirty-minute yoga class, Selma was exhausted. Tony let her lean on his broad shoulders as they walked out of the gym. Selma hesitated at first, insisting on walking to the car without Tony's help. He had been the perfect gentleman, and it became easy for Selma to feel comfortable with him.

"I'm glad you came to the gym with me," Tony said as they pulled out of the parking lot.

"That kickboxing class was plain torture," Selma said.

"It gets better if you continue," Tony said. Selma took a quick look at him. Seeing Tony as a strong man was reassuring because he exuded the kind of confidence that nudged her heart. She jolted as Tony made a sharp turn onto Route 355. "Are you okay?"

"I'm fine," Selma said. She could not believe how flustered she was. "My mind is on the article I am working on," she lied. Tony smiled. Selma tilted her head back and closed her eyes. It seemed to be a signal for Tony to slow down. They got to Selma's house six minutes later, and Selma opened her eyes.

"You must think I'm a lousy driver," Tony said.

"No, I'm just tired," Selma replied.

"You mentioned that you were thinking about a column you were writing. Do you like writing news articles?"

"I do," Selma replied. "Having a column is a huge responsibility." She seized the opportunity to talk about her column, feeling more relaxed and enjoying Tony's company.

"I'm glad I'm getting to know you better," Tony said as he got out of the car and opened the door for Selma.

"I had a great time working out for the first time in a long time," Selma replied. "It was painful, but it was fun doing it with you." Tony held her hand.

"Maybe we could go on a real date," he said. Selma pulled away and walked ahead.

"Maybe," she replied nonchalantly.

Kendra and Latisha were watching an episode of *iCarly* on Nickelodeon in the living room when Selma and Tony arrived.

"Hi, Dad, how was your workout?" Latisha asked with a mischievous stare.

"Mom, you look very tired," Kendra added. Selma went into

the kitchen and returned with two bottles of water. She gave one to Tony. He thanked her and headed toward the door.

"Latisha, we need to get going," he said. Latisha gave Kendra a quick hug.

"Thanks again for taking me to the gym," Selma said.

"Any time, Selma," Tony replied. When Latisha and Tony left, Kendra asked Selma if she liked Tony. At first Selma was defensive, but she understood how persistent Kendra could be.

"He seems nice," Selma replied. "I need to get some work done for tomorrow." Kendra raised her eyebrow. She knew better than to stay on a subject when her mother had deliberately changed to another.

Selma and Tony went on two dates, and went to the gym one more time. Selma struggled with the idea of dating after being single for so long. She didn't want to relinquish her independence and relearn to trust another man. Yet, she had called Julie after her first date with Tony, and Julie was ecstatic to hear about it.

"It's about time, Selma," Julie told her. She reasoned that the transition was easy because Kendra and Latisha were friends. Her call to Habibah did not go as well, and she began to think that Habibah might be jealous of her relationship with Tony. It was unlike Habibah to snap and accuse her of being insensitive to others.

"All you care about is your career, and nothing or nobody else," cried Habibah. Selma listened and did not respond. She tried to think about what she might have done to Habibah. One thing was clear to her. Habibah was beginning to feel overwhelmed by Christie's marital problems and Afi's family crisis. She was in the middle of everything.

The days that followed were hectic because Selma had to shop and cook for Afi's baby shower. She pondered her conversation with Christie the day she picked her from the airport. Christie did not show the kind of excitement Selma had expected when she told her about Tony. It made sense that Christie would not be enthused about Selma's relationship with Tony since Christie was going through a divorce. It occurred to Selma that she might lose her best friend because of Tony, and she had to wonder what it would be like having Tony in her life and losing her friendships with Habibah and Christie. It didn't seem plausible that a man would come between her and her friends. Julie seemed to have accepted Tony, but it would take Christie and Habibah some time to warm up to him.

Afi's baby shower was going to bring them together, and it could be a beginning or the end of their friendship. She looked forward to meeting at Christie's house to celebrate Max's birth. More than that, it was a way to meet and rejoice with their friend who almost lost her husband. With her column in mind, Selma thought about the changes that occurred in the lives of women her age.

As Selma lay in bed that night, she thought a lot about Tony and contemplated what might be the most desirable outcome. Thoughts of finding love, losing loved ones, and anticipating a long period of empty nest syndrome swirled around her mind. She often imagined her life after Kendra's high school graduation and felt the trepidation of living alone.

FIFTEEN

Selma and Kendra had finished loading the car with the food she was taking to Christie's house when Julie called to let her know she was on her way. Habibah had called earlier to say that she was taking some decorations to Christie's home. Selma arrived at Christie's house a few minutes before Julie did. Habibah and Christie helped to bring the food in.

Christie's living room was beautifully decorated with balloons and flowers. A big banner that read *Welcome Max* hung next to *The Wave* painting. Most of the paper decorations were blue. The music featured some popular Nigerian Christian songs by Agatha Moses. Kendra went down to the basement with MJ.

"This place looks great," Julie said. "Christie and Habibah, you have outdone yourselves." Christie and Julie rearranged the food on the long rectangular table. A three-layered chocolate cake, decorated with brown and a blue ribbon, was in the middle. The smallest cake was on the top, and it had *Max* written on the side. Next to the table was a big gift basket loaded with several baby items—two pacifiers, plastic keys, bibs, a blue teddy bear, and baby towels. The other presents included a fancy keepsake box, hair accessories, and some electronic baby gadgets from Leap Frog. A special basket meant for Afi and Logan included a variety of teas and cookies and a gift certificate to Massage Envy Spa. On the opposite side of the table was a baby stroller.

Selma was setting the coffee table for a game when Cynthia Bridges walked in.

"Hello, everyone," she said as she placed a bag on the sofa. She wore a pink Mariposa maxi dress and a sterling silver necklace.

"Hi, Cynthia," Selma said. "I'm so glad you could make it."

"Thank you for inviting me," Cynthia replied. "The food smells delicious, and I can't wait to try everything!"

"I'd like you to meet my friends, Christie, Julie, and Habibah," Selma said. "Cynthia Bridges is a friend and a co-worker at the *Gazette*."

"Welcome," the three women chorused.

"Thank you for having me," Cynthia replied as she sat in the recliner. Christie went upstairs to get ready while Julie and Selma continued to set up game pieces on the coffee table. Habibah brought the punch she made to the big table. Julie's quesadillas were a good addition to the rice, bean cakes, and fried plantains.

A gray Honda pulled to the curb behind Christie's mailbox. "They're here," Julie announced. Christie came downstairs dressed in a green brocade caftan. Elaine Fisher emerged from the driver's side and helped Afi bring out the baby carrier. Afi's mother, Mawusi, removed the diaper bag from the backseat. Afi stood wide-eyed looking at the elaborate decorations for her surprise baby shower. She stared at the cake and was speechless.

"My goodness, you ladies went all out for this," Elaine said.

"Afi, you are really blessed to have friends like this," Mawusi said as she adjusted her purple lace wrapper. Afi placed the baby carrier in the chair and sat at the edge. Kendra and MJ emerged from the basement and went toward the baby.

"Welcome," Christie said. "Please make yourself at home." She seemed to enjoy hosting the baby shower for Afi. It was a good distraction from her next court hearing. Having Julie as Christie's lawyer seemed weird at first, but Selma assured her that Julie understood her role as her lawyer and as her friend. Julie was helping to prepare her case to retain the house and custody of MJ. Martin had recruited a family attorney from the Williams and Watson law firm. Mr. Mark Watson represented him, and Julie couldn't be happier. She has been opposite Watson before and was excited about another match up with him during Christie's court hearings.

"Congratulation, Afi," Cynthia said.

"Cynthia, I'd like you to meet my daughter, Kendra," Selma said. Kendra shook her hand and went to get some food. MJ joined her and the two went back to the basement.

"We should be getting ready to eat," Habibah said. She has been unusually quiet; clearly something was not right with her. Afi removed the baby from his carrier, and Elaine sat next to her, attending to baby needs.

Christie increased the volume of the African music on her CD player. Julie stood and started dancing. Mawusi joined in, and Cynthia followed. Afi tried to soothe the baby, who was crying louder because of the noise. Selma had not seen this boisterous side of Cynthia. Even though it was her first time meeting Selma's friends, Cynthia felt right at home.

"Selma, this is a great party, thank you for inviting me," Cynthia said.

"It is nice meeting you," Julie said.

"I already feel like one of you. How did you all meet?" Cynthia asked.

"Julie was Selma's divorce attorney and she is representing me now," Christie said. "Habibah and Afi are my friends and we are nurses."

"Are you co-workers?" Cynthia asked

"All three of us worked at NIH, but Habibah left NIH and now works at private practice clinic," Afi said.

"And I am Selma's colleague at the *Gazette*," Cynthia said.

"Afi's mother, Mawusi, is visiting from Africa, and Elaine is Afi's mother-in-law," Habibah added.

"Friendship is the greatest gift we can give each other," Elaine said.

"Thank you for this beautiful party," Afi said. "Logan and I are very grateful to all of you. I don't know what I would have done without you." Afi's voice choked.

"You have come a long way, Afi," Selma said. Afi closed her eyes and tears dropped. Selma patted her on the back. There was a knock on the door. Christie brought fried pastry from the kitchen and placed it on the table before answering the door. Two women Selma had never met wiped their feet and walked in.

"Christie, you have a beautiful home," the first one said as she walked in.

"Thank you, Sandra," Christie replied. "Please make yourself comfortable."

"Thank you for inviting us," the second woman added. Afi grinned and her face lit up when she noticed the newcomers.

"I don't know what to say," Afi stammered. Christie introduced Sandra and the second woman, Rosetta, as coworkers, and ushered them to the empty seats next to the Elaine and Mawusi.

"Do you all work in the same department at NIH?" Julie inquired as she walked back to her seat with a plate of food.

"Rosetta and I work at the Clinical Rehabilitation Center," Afi replied.

"I work with Christie in clinical research," Sandra said.

"Please get something to eat," Elaine said in a motherly tone. Christie raised the music's volume again.

Selma and Afi stood and danced to Nigerian gospel singer

Agatha Moses, and Julie joined in.

"Selma, you must invite me to another event like this," Cynthia said as she joined the dance. Julie took out her phone and started filming when Rosetta and Sandra started dancing as well. The mood was festive and uplifting. Elaine watched with pride as she held her grandson. Habibah and Elaine cheered. The party lasted for almost two hours. Mawusi could hardly contain her joy when she saw all the presents.

"I don't know what to say," Mawusi said. "My name means 'In God's hands,' and I know my daughter, her family and all her friends are in God's hands."

"I am very lucky to have you in my life," Afi said. She paused to hold back tears. "I cannot thank you enough for all your support during my pregnancy and after my husband got shot." She hugged Selma and then Christie.

"Do not underestimate the power of friendship among ladies," Selma said. "We are a pack of mama bears, and we know how to take care of our own."

The music ended, and it was time to leave. Afi helped Elaine place the baby in the carrier while Kendra helped load up their car with the presents. Cynthia hugged Selma and stood to leave.

"It's been nice meeting all of you." Cynthia said. "I now realize how lucky I am to be working with Selma."

Habibah started the dishwasher and put away the pots and pans. Selma and Christie cleaned the living room and put away all the leftover food. When they had finally finished, they all sat on the sofa completely exhausted. Selma thought it was a good time to find out what was bothering Habibah.

"I have something to tell you," Habibah started. Christie and Selma leaned forward and waited.

"Whatever it is, I hope you know we're here for you," Selma said.

"Last week I had a mammogram, and they discovered a

lump in my right breast." She spoke slowly. "My doctor ordered a biopsy."

"And what was the result?" Christie asked anxiously.

"The initial result indicated that it is cancerous, but my doctor wants us to wait until the final result comes back on Tuesday."

"That's when you will know for sure, right?" Christie asked.

"Yes," Habibah nodded. "You know my mom died of breast cancer, right?"

"We know, but it doesn't mean you will die," Christie said. "You are going to fight it like nothing else matters."

"Habibah, we will always be here for you," Selma said. "You take care of everybody; I hope you will let us take care of you." Habibah held her hand and nodded.

"What is the next step?" Christie asked.

"I really don't know," Habibah replied. "I guess we will have to wait and see."

"You will let us know as soon as you hear anything, right?" Christie said.

"You will be the first to know," Habibah replied. She fought back tears and hugged Christie and Selma. "Only you guys can put up with this grouchy me." Selma winked.

"You promised to let us take care of you, and you have to keep to it," Selma said. "I want to you to face this cancer head on, and we will be there with you all the way." Selma was focused on solving the problem.

"Have you told your son and your brothers?" Christie asked.

"I have told my son because he is here with me, and I must say that he is my rock." Habibah's voice quivered. She could feel her throat tighten. Christie reached for the Kleenex box and pulled tissues for Habibah. "I have not told my brothers. I will tell them after I get the results of the biopsy."

"Between Selma, Julie, Afi and me, there will always be

someone to go to your appointments with you," Christie said. Their bond seemed even stronger. Selma nodded as Christie assured Habibah of their support.

Kendra came up from the basement and got a water from the refrigerator.

"Mom, can we go home now?" she asked. Habibah rose and went to the bathroom as Selma assented and gathered her dishes.

"Habibah is really going to need us," Christie said to Selma.

"Why does this have to happen to Habibah?" Selma asked as if there were an answer.

"I have come to a conclusion that life just isn't fair," Christie concurred. Habibah returned from the bathroom and announced that she was leaving. Selma and Habibah left at the same time.

Selma called Tony just before she went to bed and told him about Habibah. Divulging her vulnerability did not seem right at first, but she soon realized how much she needed him. One thing became clear to her that night. Friends were indispensable. Maybe it was God's way of letting humanity know how helpless and interdependent everyone really was.

She took an inventory of the ideas she had expressed in her column about women, their losses as well as their triumphs. Habibah's battle with cancer gave her a new perspective of the challenges that women like her faced. She imagined what she would do if she were Habibah.

SIXTEEN

Habibah's cancer diagnosis weighed heavily on Selma as she drove to work. Her initial reaction was to find a solution. In her mind, there had to be a way to fix this. The fear of death, especially the death of a friend, overwhelmed her. She had lost a childhood friend at the age of twelve. Even though she did not fully understand the finality of death at that age, she remembered wishing that she had died with her friend. Losing Habibah would be devastating, and she was not going to let it happen.

Selma also thought about Christie on the drive. Her friend's preliminary divorce hearing had not gone well. Christie had sold her condominium when she married Martin, and since her name was not on the original contract of their present house, Martin requested that they sell it. He reminded the judge that he bought the house before he married Christie. Julie had argued that it was marital property, but the judge did not agree. Moving to a smaller house was going to be big adjustment for Christie.

At the office, Selma caught Blackwell placing his hand on his forehead and showing obvious signs of pain as he walked past.

"Are you okay?" Selma asked.

"Just a headache that just won't quit," he replied. "I was up working on an editorial on the plans to move Walter Reed Medical Center from Washington to Bethesda."

"I hope you feel better," Selma said.

"A few extra hours of sleep would help tremendously," Blackwell said with a grin. "Thank you for your concern, Selma."

Moving Walter Reed to Bethesda was, in Blackwell's view, a bad move because of its proximity to NIH and the traffic congestion in the area. In his article he pointed out that Congress was playing Russian roulette by ignoring the safety of pedestrians and motorists.

Selma had just turned on her computer and opened her emails when Jaden stopped by. She was not expecting him, since their recent collaborations on various articles had been mostly by email. Jaden had not made any attempts to apologize for his outburst, and Selma made a conscious decision to work with him and be professional in spite of his animosity toward her. She was convinced that Jaden was threatened by her seeming success, and it did not surprise her. To her it looked like his male ego getting in the way, yet she admired his work ethic and his attention to detail.

"Good morning, Selma," Jaden said. Selma raised her eyebrows in surprise.

"Good morning, Jaden," she replied. "I am just about to check my email to see what we should be working on.

"I haven't sent one yet," Jaden replied. "Is it okay if I sit and talk with you for a minute?"

"Sure," Selma replied.

"This is late, but it's better late than never," Jaden began. Selma listened intently. "I apologize for acting like a jerk." Selma dropped her head and waited. "Did you hear me? Feel free to call me a jerk." He paused and stared at Selma.

"I heard you, Jaden," Selma replied. "I accept your apology." Jaden forced a smile. "You know something? I really admire you for how well you carry yourself around here."

"That means a lot, Selma," Jaden said. "I would say the same thing about you, especially how you have stayed focused on your dream and made it a reality right before my eyes." Selma grinned.

"You are making it difficult for me to stay mad at you," she said. "In a lot of ways you remind me of my little brother, CJ."

Gary's voice cut through the air and startled Jaden and Selma.

"Someone call an ambulance immediately!" he screamed. "Call 911!" Jaden and Selma hurried toward Gary's office and saw Blackwell's door was wide open. Gary knelt beside him shaking him frantically. Blackwell struggled to breathe. Jaden loosened his tie.

"I've got this," Jaden said. "I know CPR." Selma bit her lower lip and paced back and forth. She whispered a prayer and watched at Jaden performed chest compressions. When the EMTs and paramedics arrived Blackwell's breathing was still irregular, and he was sweating profusely.

"He's having cardiac arrest," one of the paramedics said. He took over the chest compression from Jaden while the other paramedic checked Blackwell's vital signs.

The intensity of the process scared Selma. She watched as the three paramedics placed Steve on the gurney and wheeled him towards the ambulance.

Selma returned to her desk. The news feed was streaming the story of Prince William and Kate Middleton's engagement. Jaden emailed Selma asking her to follow the story and write reactions to the news. There was a barrage of breaking news as reactions poured in about the royal engagement. Jaden returned to Blackwell's office to look over the Walter Reed Medical Center editorial. Cynthia returned to her office to complete her article on the North Korean nuclear program. In spite of the commotion, everyone seemed concerned about returning to some kind normalcy at the *Gazette*. Jaden had his phone in one hand as he checked Blackwell's article. He anxiously waited for word from the hospital about the boss's condition. Gary called Jaden an hour later to alert him that Blackwell's wife and son were at the hospital and said Blackwell suffered a massive heart attack. Steve Blackwell died a few minutes before midnight.

Gary returned to the office shortly just before noon. He went directly to his office and did not speak to anyone. Jaden talked to Lisa and Arianna about writing Blackwell's obituary. Though the mood at the *Gazette* was somber, death did not change or slow down the work. The news business was a revolving door, and Selma had to learn to make sense of what came in and went out. She pondered the brief conversation she had with Blackwell that morning. It was hard to believe that Lisa and Arianna were writing his obituary less than six hours later.

Selma turned off her radio during her drive home. A tidal wave of questions bombarded her, and they were questions she could not find answers for. *What will happen to Habibah? Will I be writing about her in past tense? What about Christie?*

Selma hugged Kendra tightly when she got home and told her that she needed some time alone. Kendra asked if she was okay. Selma nodded and hugged Kendra again before going to her room.

The mood in the office was still somber the next morning. Gary did a second edit of Blackwell's editorial and had it ready for publication. Jaden and Curtis took a final look at the obituary before posting it on the print version of the paper. For Selma, the minutes and hours dragged on and made the day seem twice as long.

Selma called Habibah before she left her office. She had arranged to accompany her to her CT scan appointment and needed to confirm. Her sadness made her more determined than ever to support Habibah in her fight against breast cancer. She could not help wondering if Blackwell's death could have been prevented. *Were there signs that were ignored? Did the paramedics and doctors miss anything in trying to save his life? What will happen to his family? What would happen to Kendra and to my family if I died suddenly?*

Kendra got home early to heat up some Stouffer's lasagna. She was determined to cheer her mother up because it was clear that something was bothering her. The mixed aroma of garlic, oregano and basil filled the kitchen and the living room when Selma arrived. She could hear Kendra singing Toby Mac's "Me Without You," along with the clinking and clanging of pots and pans. Selma sank into the sofa and stretched out.

"Hi, Kendra," Selma said.

"Welcome home, Mom. I'm heating lasagna for dinner."

"Thank you so much, Kendra."

"I made your favorite salad as well," Kendra said. Selma smiled and shook her head.

"You never cease to amaze me, Kendra." She rose and went into the kitchen. Kendra set the table while Selma dished out the food.

"Mom, I know something was bothering you yesterday, and I wanted to do something for you," Kendra said. Selma looked at her. At that moment, she felt proud of her daughter for her sensitivity.

"You remind me of my mother, Kendra," Selma said. "I appreciate you making dinner." They finished eating, and Selma rose to take her plate to the sink.

"Don't worry, Mom," Kendra said as she took the plates from her mother. "Dinner is on me, and I will clean up as well." The house phone rang.

"Thank you, Kendra," Selma said as she hurried into the

living room to answer the call. After informing Christie about Steve's death, Selma was overcome by anguish and a sense of helplessness. She began to sob. Kendra rushed out of the kitchen, befuddled by her mom's grief. Christie had hung up the phone when she heard nothing but crying on the line.

"What is the matter, Mom?" Kendra asked as she sat next to her mother. Selma pulled Kendra closer and hugged her tightly. This was a side of her mother that was not familiar to her. "Should I call Tony?"

"Don't worry, Kendra. I'll be okay." She removed a small packet of tissue from her bag and wiped her face. Kendra always saw her mother as an independent, invincible woman, who took charge and could face any problem. It was unusual and upsetting to see her so powerless.

"What happened?" Kendra asked.

"One of my colleagues died unexpectedly" Selma replied.

"I am so sorry, Mom," Kendra said. Selma wiped her eyes and blew her nose. She walked to the window and noticed Christie pulling into the space next to her car. She went to the door and opened it for Christie.

"What is the matter?" Christie said as soon as she entered.

"I'm sorry I dragged you here," Selma said. "My boss had a massive heart attack and died unexpectedly." Christie hugged her and patted her back.

"I am so sorry to hear this," Christie said. "Is this is the funny Italian guy who writes funny articles?

"Not Gary," Selma replied. "It was my boss, Steven Blackwell." They sat at the dining table. Selma had a blank look on her face. Christie held her hand and tried to console her. Kendra emerged from the kitchen holding a spatula.

"Hi, Auntie Christie," Kendra said.

"Hello, Kendra! It looks like you're cooking dinner," said Christie.

"I made lasagna and Caesar salad, and we've already eaten dinner," Kendra replied proudly.

"It must have been delicious," Christie said. Selma forced a smile and glanced at her daughter. Kendra hurried back to the kitchen.

"Where is MJ?" Selma asked.

"He's at the playground with one of my neighbor's kids," Christie replied.

"Mom, your phone is ringing." Kendra called out. "You left it in the kitchen." Selma gave Christie's hand a gentle squeeze and stood up to get her phone. Christie noticed Tony walking toward the house, holding a bouquet of pink roses. Latisha walked closely behind him. Selma's phone call with Habibah was short. Selma told her that she would call her back. She opened the front door for Tony and Latisha. Christie and Selma exchanged quick glances as Tony gave Selma the roses. Latisha waved at Christie and Selma and went into the kitchen. Tony hugged Selma.

"Christie, meet Tony Harris, a friend," Selma said. Christie raised her eyebrows. "Tony, meet one of my best friends, Christie." Tony reached out and shook Christie's hand.

"Thank you for the flowers, Tony," Selma said.

"Kendra sent Latisha a text about the passing of your boss," Tony said.

"Thank you, Tony," Selma said. Christie watched Tony and Selma and wondered how this possible romance would change Selma's relationship with Christie and perhaps her career. Christie knew how much Selma's career meant to her; getting into a relationship with Tony was a bit of a surprise. She recalled that Selma's divorce happened at the onset of her own relationship with Martin. She noticed how Tony looked at Selma, and she began to draw conclusions.

"I guess I should be leaving now," said Christie.

"Would you like something to eat?" Selma asked Christie.

"How about some rice with fried plantains."

"I need to get MJ from my neighbor," Christie replied. Kendra came out of the kitchen just as Christie opened the door to leave.

"This holiday season is beginning to look bleak for me," Selma said after Christie left. "I would like to start planning a Christmas party and have everyone here because it is important." Kendra noticed Tony's troubled look. Tony apparently did not like the idea of Selma's friends joining her for Christmas dinner.

"Who are you planning to invite to the Christmas party, Mom?" Kendra asked.

"With less than a month to plan it, I need to start as soon as possible," Selma said. Tony excused himself and went to the bathroom.

"Would you like some ice cream?" Kendra asked Latisha.

"Sure," Latisha replied. She followed Kendra to the kitchen. Selma walked to the window. It was already dark outside, and for a minute, she indulged in the beauty of the evolving small town. Tony returned a few minutes later and announced that they would be leaving.

"Is anything the matter?" Selma asked. Kendra stood at the kitchen door and watched. Latisha put on her sandals and waited at the door.

"No, oh no," replied Tony. "It's been a long day. I know you need your rest too." Selma shrugged and watched Tony and Latisha leave. Kendra wondered why she had not noticed Tony's uneasiness.

"Mom, do you like Tony?" Kendra asked as she washed the dishes.

"Why did you ask? Are you worried that I will not give you the attention you deserve?"

"I just don't want you to get hurt again," Kendra replied.

"Honey, are you upset about something?" Selma said as she placed her hand on her shoulder. Kendra did not respond. "You know you can tell me anything."

"I don't have a good feeling about him," Kendra said. Selma hugged her.

"I am glad you are telling me how you feel, Kendra," Selma said. "You don't have to worry about us." Kendra pulled away gently. Selma turned to leave.

"Mom, you care so much about the people you love," Kendra said. "You have taught me to care about other people too." Selma smiled. Kendra closed the dishwasher and rinsed her hands.

"I can't tell you how proud you have made me," Selma said as they walked into the living room. "You need to know that I will never put anybody's needs above yours." Kendra nodded. Selma kissed her on the forehead before letting her go. Kendra went upstairs, but Selma decided to relax on the sofa for a while. She realized that she had not checked her dating status for over two days. Her article was almost complete, but she could still get messages for article.

Selma took an inventory of the articles she had written and reflected on what impact they might have had. In three short months she had been involved in writing a breaking news story about a shooting that almost claimed the life of a friend. She had worked hard enough to impress her once skeptical boss. Working as an investigative reporter seemed exciting at first, but it soon became a test of her patience since she had to invest time and effort to gather the information she needed to write and report the story.

Selma thought about the recent events in her life. She realized that Blackwell's funeral had been scheduled on the same day as Habibah's doctor's appointment. She needed to be at both.

Kendra came back into the living room and sat next to Selma on the sofa. Selma held Kendra's hand and squeezed it gently.

"Sometimes I wonder what I'd do without you," Selma said. "You have grown very quickly, and you are taking care of yourself and taking care of me as well."

"You raised me well, Mother," Kendra replied. Selma leaned towards Kendra. "Mom."

"What is it?" Selma asked. She noticed the serious look on Kendra's face.

"Latisha told me something in the kitchen." Kendra paused. "She likes you a lot."

"And?" Selma's eyes were wide open as she stared at Kendra.

"She just said that she hopes her dad does not mess this up again," Kendra replied.

"I don't want you to worry about Tony, okay?" Selma reassured Kendra.

"I just want you to be happy, and I want us to be safe as well," Kendra said as she stood to leave.

"Kendra, I promise you that I will jeopardize our safety for anything or anyone," Selma said.

"Okay," Kendra replied. "I need to go to bed now." She walked upstairs as Selma got up to check the front door.

Selma wondered what impact Blackwell's death would have on the *Gazette*. Most of the writers and editors at the *Gazette* had relied on his guidance and judgment. His legacy as an edgy journalist who had no qualms about taking on even the most controversial political or social issue was indisputable. Gary's satirical style was a good compliment to Blackwell's forceful editorials.

Less than an hour later, Selma could hear Kendra breathing heavily. She found the door to her room ajar. She closed it gently and returned to her room. She thought about what Kendra told her. Tony seemed like a decent man, but she began to realize that he might not have been completely honest. *Does he have a dark side? Is he possessive?* She tossed and turned, letting her mind wander.

SEVENTEEN

Four days after the sudden death of Blackwell, the writers and editors at the *Gazette* gradually adjusted, some taking on new roles. Selma got to the office about five minutes before the emergency staff meeting. Jaden had been working more closely with Gary and took up a leadership role at the office. Selma read Jaden's email announcing that a new writer had been hired to help fill the void left by Blackwell. Even though Jaden told Selma that her position might change, she took comfort in the fact that she would still retain her column. Cynthia had shown an interest in Gary's position, but she preferred the opportunity to travel and continue her job as the international correspondent. She had been invited to be part of the interview panel for a new staff writer at the *Gazette*.

An email went out to Cynthia, Gary and Jaden from Laura Blackwell, asking them to write short tributes to read at her husband's funeral. Selma had started a column about dealing with tragic situations and maintaining an even higher level of friendship among women in their forties. Her premise for this idea was Habibah's cancer diagnosis. Ideally, families, especially spouses, were the primary caregivers of loved ones who had debilitating illnesses like cancer. The reality for women like Habibah, Christie and Selma herself, because of the change in their family circumstances, was that they had to rely on their friends and, in some cases, the kindness of strangers. She started the lead paragraph and needed to complete the article that day.

Gary, Jaden, Cynthia, and Curtis had converged in the conference room for the emergency staff meeting when Selma arrived. Gary sat at the head of the table and next to him was a tall athletically-built African-American man. He wore a black business suit and gray striped shirt. His short brown hair was neatly combed to the left side and his beard was short and trimmed. Selma sat between Cynthia and Jaden. She glanced at the new guy and noticed his stern look and all-business demeanor. He did not seem to have anything in common with Gary. Jaden asked him about his work ethics, while Gary asked him about how well he worked as a team member. His response to the questions convinced Selma that he would be a good addition to the *Gazette*. Gary had everyone meet again right after lunch.

Gary addressed the group with a few lighthearted jokes to lighten the tense mood in the room. Cynthia leaned back in her chair and stared at Gary as they waited for him to make the announcement.

"I would like to introduce Jeffery Taylor, our newest staff member." After a short round of applause, Gary continued. "Jeff will be taking over from Selma." Selma swallowed the lump in her throat. Cynthia eyes were wide open as she waited for the rest of the announcements. She was on the previous interview panel and had been in favor of another candidate, a three-year correspondent for the *Washington Post*. Jeffery cleared his throat and placed his hand on the table. Nobody moved or even made a sound.

"I will start by offering my condolences for your loss," Jeffery said. "I am delighted to be a part of a very successful news organization." The silence in the room was deafening. "I was born in Baltimore, but I have spent most my career here in the DC metro area." Selma's mind was racing as it became clear that she would end up working with Jeffery. In addition to an impressive resume that included a year on Wall Street and two years as staff writer for *Time* magazine, Jeffery exuded an erudite personality. Selma nodded. Although she knew how reluctant she could be about change, she had no doubt that she could work with anyone just as well as she did with Gary and Jaden.

Gary concluded the meeting by explaining that he would be working more closely with Jaden. Then Gary announced that Selma was going to be taking over for Jaden.

Selma's jaw dropped. With Jeffery's impressive resume and work experience, she was almost sure that he would be taking Jaden's place and not the other way round. She knew that Gary had made the decision to give her more responsibilities because, from the onset, Gary believed in her ability to accept change and grow. The meeting ended after a few short speeches to welcome Jeffery.

Selma led Jeffery to her cubicle and assured him that she planned to move into Jaden's office the following week, and he could move into her space.

"I look forward to working with you," Jeffery said.

"Same here, Jeffery," Selma replied.

"Please call me Jeff," he said. Selma smiled. Cynthia walked over to welcome Jeff, and encouraged him to feel at home.

There were signs of Christmas all over the area as Blackwell's family prepared for his funeral, which would be two weeks from Christmas day. Street decorations and the abundance of sales to attract holiday shoppers covered major streets and media outlets. Selma wrote a short tribute and hurried out of the building to take Habibah to her PET-scan appointment. She felt a mild headache as she got into her car. The past few weeks had been hectic; as much as she thought she had total control of the circumstances surrounding her, she had to admit that the stress was taking its toll.

Selma got a text from Kendra, all in capital letters as she pulled out of the parking lot. *COME HOME NOW! IT IS IMPORTANT.*

She thought about calling Kendra, but she decided to rush home before taking Habibah to her appointment. She called and told Habibah that she may be running late. Kendra opened the door for Selma when she got home.

"What is going on?" Selma asked. She noticed Kendra's laptop on the coffee table.

"This," Kendra said, and showed her the newsfeed on her computer screen. It seemed odd that Kendra would read or listen to the news.

"What?" Selma asked. On the screen was a photograph of Tony—a wanted fugitive. "What?" Selma mouthed. She listened to the video report from an NBC affiliate in Orlando, Florida.

"A decorated war veteran is wanted for the murder of his estranged wife," the reporter said. She stood in front of a modest house with a single-car garage next to a small lake. "Mr. Nelson Wright lived in this house behind me with his estranged wife and a daughter who has gone missing."

Selma was dumbfounded. She looked at Kendra and back to the news and caught the last part.

"Mr. Wright may be traveling with his teenage daughter around the Northeast. He is considered armed and dangerous." Selma swallowed a lump in her throat. She starred at Kendra with her mouth open for a minute and then back on the screen. The headline was unequivocal: *Decorated Veteran Now a Fugitive Wanted for Murder.* Kendra raised her eyebrows. She saw her mother's reaction and knew she didn't have to say anything. Selma took a deep breath and looked at her watch.

"I need to take Auntie Habibah to the doctor. Please be careful around Latisha," Selma cautioned. "Don't say anything to her." Kendra nodded. "You know what—do not let her in the house until I get home."

Habibah was her usual jovial self when Selma arrived to take her to her appointment. Selma wondered if she had found out something and was not telling her. Perhaps Habibah's emotions were on an upswing or she was just having a very good day. She could also be in denial about the tough recovery road ahead. Whatever it was, Selma was glad to see Habibah in good spirits after the shocking discovery of Tony's lies. She imagined how he would take the news that she knew who he was and was aware that he was a fugitive. She was going to tell Habibah and Christie about Tony, but she knew that right now she had to focus on Habibah and support her.

An older nurse called Habibah in for her preliminary tests and vitals before the scan. She told Selma to stay in the waiting room.

"Are you a family member?" she asked Selma. She had a Caribbean accent. Her hair was pulled back to form a bun. It was almost completely gray.

"I am her friend," Selma replied. She turned to Habibah and whispered, "It will be okay." The nurse led her past the double steel doors. Selma caught a glimpse of Habibah's face as she walked into the changing room and noticed her teary eyes. Habibah was very good at hiding her emotions, but Selma could tell that she was terrified. She stood up immediately and asked the nurse behind the counter if she could go in. The nurse smiled and beckoned her through the steel doors.

The door of the second room was ajar, and the nurse waited for Habibah, who was changing into a blue hospital robe. Habibah's mouth gaped open in disbelief when she saw Selma. She held Selma's hands and nodded before hopping onto the exam table. Selma watched the nurse take Habibah's temperature and blood pressure. The nurse assured Selma and Habibah that the vital signs were good.

A man in a white lab coat with a stethoscope around his neck walked into the room holding an open manila folder. Selma stood up and shook his hand. Habibah took a deep breath and smiled with tight lips.

"Hello, I am Dr. Franklin. How are you doing, Ms. Habibah?" Dr. Franklin placed the folder on the counter.

"Dr. Franklin, hello," Habibah replied. Her stoic expression could not be missed. Selma nodded and gave her a reassuring smile.

"Most of your blood test results are in," said Dr. Franklin. Habibah's eyes were fixed on him. "Based on these preliminary tests, the biomarkers are evident and indicate the presence of a tumor."

"How do we know if the cancer is still contained and has not gone anywhere else?" Selma asked.

"That is a very good question," Dr. Franklin replied. "Habibah's oncologist will read the rest of the blood tests and will most likely run a series of tests to learn more about the tumor." He noticed the distressed look on Habibah's face.

"What is your gut feeling about Habibah's situation?" Selma asked.

"I have reason to believe that this cancer is still at the early stage," Dr. Franklin replied. "Whenever cancer is diagnosed at its early stage, the patient has a very good chance of beating it." Selma nodded. "Her treatment may include a mastectomy, radiation or chemotherapy, but her oncologist would determine the best treatment for her."

"So we just have to wait to see what the oncologist decides," Selma said.

"Yes," replied Dr. Franklin. "I will check on you after you see Dr. Gilbert."

"There is also a chance that I will have the surgery as well as the radiation and chemotherapy, right?" Habibah asked.

"Yes," Dr. Franklin replied. "It depends on the nature of the cancer and the best treatment for it."

Habibah understood the routine. With a cancer diagnosis, it was a long course of treatments that would likely include surgery. As Selma and Habibah walked out the building, Habibah expressed a renewed sense of determination to do whatever it took to fight the disease.

"I just hate to wait," Habibah exclaimed as she got into Selma's car. The results were going to be sent to her oncologist and she would find out within a day or two.

"I don't like waiting either, but whatever lesson we need to learn, I hope we learn it," Selma said. Habibah kept a blank face. "Habibah, you know you have to do what you need to do to get better." Habibah nodded. "Sometimes it is okay to cry," said Selma. "Your friends are here for you."

"I know I have to be strong for my son," Habibah added. "I'm all he's got." She choked.

"I understand," Selma said calmly.

They drove in silence the rest of the way. Selma thought about praying and about the power of positive thinking. Even at an early age, she took time to rationalize her thinking regarding faith and what to believe. In her mind, praying required faith and faith meant a positive outlook. Whatever the case, she knew that she needed both.

Selma was able to drop off Habibah and make it to Steve's service. She had time to stop for a small smoothie.

The melodious voice of a female vocalist singing "Beneath Your Wings" cut through the stillness of Grace Episcopal Church. Parishioners, family members, friends and colleagues made their way into the majestic building for Steve's funeral. Steven Blackwell had served on the church elder board for eight years. The entire staff of the *Uptown Gazette* sat in the front left side of the church, along with family members, including Laura Blackwell and her children. Pastel flowers covered the mahogany casket.

Reverend Anderson preached a short sermon about Steve Blackwell's legacy. The mourners shared tributes and memories. Gary's tribute changed the somber atmosphere.

"In case you wonder what this Italian Jewish boy is doing in a beautiful church, wonder no more." Gary paused and waited for the chuckles to die down. He continued after a few claps, referring to Steve as a mentor and a friend. Jaden read a short poem he called an "Ode to a Gentle Giant." Jaden was known among his peers as a man of very few words. In his poem, he credited Steve for teaching him to reflect on everything he wrote and referred to him as his "comfort rock." For her part, Cynthia referred to Steve as a friend and colleague who made her strive to be her best. Selma was glad that she got a chance to talk about Steve. She talked about Steve's humility and grace. Without purposely alluding to her first meeting with Steve, Selma talked about Blackwell as a boss who cared deeply about people. She talked about him coming to her cubicle to applaud her for the success of her column. Blackwell was laid to rest in a cemetery behind the church later that day.

EIGHTEEN

Gladys was the first to arrive in class for the final exam. Selma removed the contents of the big brown envelope and wrote directions on the board. She placed a stack of pencils on the desk and began passing out the exams. Tyrone was absent. Gladys gazed at the ceiling and at the floor. She squinted and read a passage in the exam packet closely. Tyrone stormed into the classroom and picked up an exam packet and pencil from the table. Selma watched as he sat upright, smiling and nodding as he read the text. He completed the exam forty-five minutes later and thanked Selma before he left. Gladys was the last person to leave. Selma walked to the window a few times and stared outside. She looked at the clock on the wall and at Gladys, who was still engrossed in her test.

"I'm sorry I kept you so long," Gladys said as she handed her exam to Selma ten minutes later.

"That's okay. I hope you did well," Selma replied. She gathered the test packets and answer sheets.

"I will never forget you, professor," Gladys said. "Thank you for all your help." Selma smiled and patted her on the back.

"Gladys, I like your determination and hard work," Selma said. "I wish you the very best." Gladys picked up her backpack and left. Selma packed up the exam materials and placed them in the big brown envelope. As she reached in her purse for her keys, her phone vibrated. It was Julie calling to ask if Selma planned to stop by her house. Selma demurred.

"I've decided to have that Christmas party after all," Selma said. She and Kendra were going to clean and decorate the house for the party. Selma planned to stop at Sam's Club to pick up a cake. Logan and Afi were going to bring a case of wine coolers. Logan's mother, Elaine, planned to return to Texas after Christmas, but Mawusi still had three months left on her visa. She planned to provide homemade eggnog.

Julie said she planned to come with Roberto. Selma was silent for a moment. She could tell that there was more to the story.

"Is there anything you're not telling me?" Selma asked.

"What do you mean?"

"I was already expecting you to bring Roberto to the party," Selma said.

"Tony will be there, right?" Julie asked, distracting Selma.

"We need to talk," replied Selma. "Maybe I should stop by briefly."

"I am home," Julie replied.

Two hours later Selma pulled into one of the parking spaces and headed to the elevator. She noticed Roberto getting into a red Ford Focus. He pulled out before she had a chance to talk to him. Julie had left the door unlocked for Selma. They embraced when Selma entered.

"Roberto just left," Julie said.

"I saw him getting into his car," said Selma. "I hope he didn't leave because of me."

"Oh, no, he and some of his buddies have plans to watch a

soccer game," Julie said as she sat on the couch. Selma sat on the recliner across from her.

"How come you didn't go with him?" Selma asked.

"I have to prepare for a major case, and the hearing is Monday morning," Julie replied. "So what is going on with you and Tony?"

"He is not who he claims to be, Julie," Selma said and shook her head.

"No way!"

"I got carried away by his charm," Selma said. "And he was a decorated veteran, awarded a Purple Heart for saving the lives of two other solders."

"And he's not all that?" Julie cried.

"He is all that and a murderer," Selma replied. Julie's jaw dropped. "He is a fugitive wanted in Florida for the murder of his wife."

"How did you find this out?" Julie asked, still in shock.

"Kendra saw the story on the newsfeed and called me to come and see," Selma said. "His real name is Nelson Wright, and he's wanted for the murder of his wife."

"I can't believe that jerk is a criminal!" Julie said. She rose and went into the kitchen. Her cat sauntered into the living room and hopped on the couch. Julie returned with two glasses of water, but Selma couldn't stay.

"I need to get Kendra and head home," Selma said.

"I am sorry to hear about Tony," Julie said. "What are you going to do about it?"

"I have to tread this ground with caution," Selma replied. "I know I have to turn him in, but I want to live to write about it." Julie giggled.

"On a serious note, you need to turn him in before he hurts you," she cautioned. "Does he have any idea that you know his crime?"

"No, he doesn't, but I know I have to think about our safety," Selma said. "According to the news, he is armed and dangerous." Selma stood up and walked to the door.

"Please be careful," Julie said as she rose and joined Selma. "You need to be *very* careful."

"This whole thing is surreal," Selma said. "Thank you for being so understanding." She left Julie's apartment relieved that she had told someone. She had not said anything to Christie or Habibah.

Selma thought about Roberto as she drove home. Julie seemed happy with him, but Selma was still concerned about his loyalty to Julie. *Is he really going to watch soccer with his friends?* The fact that Julie, who had never been married, was involved with a much younger man concerned Selma. She believed that a young handsome stud like Roberto would take advantage of Julie and leave her for a woman his own age.

Selma and Kendra got home in time for Kendra to watch her favorite show on Nickelodeon, *iCarly*. Selma went cooked penne pasta, grilled chicken and vegetables. She and Kendra did not talk much during dinner. Kendra broke the silence when she complimented her mother on how well she made her pasta.

"Kendra, I am very proud of the way you followed your instinct and found out about Tony."

"I hope he gets caught so that he doesn't hurt someone else," Kendra replied.

"You know I have to confront Tony and notify the police, and I'm thinking that the sooner the better," Selma said. Kendra froze. "I understand that it's scary, but we have to act fast so that he doesn't hurt us."

"How about Latisha?" Kendra asked.

"Well, I am sure that they have family members who will take good care of her," Selma replied. She reassured Kendra that she would not do anything to put their lives in danger.

She called Tony after she and Kendra cleared the table. Tony agreed to come by Selma's home. It was a risk she was willing to take. Tony already knew where she lived. She took Kendra's phone and included 911 on her speed dial. When Tony asked about Kendra, Selma told him that she had to spend the night at Christie's home.

Kendra's eyes opened wide as she stared at her mother. Selma placed her finger on her lips as a signal for Kendra to be quiet.

"Yes, I am home alone," Selma said and hung up the phone.

"What did you do that for?" Kendra asked.

"Listen, you are going to stay in your room and have your phone ready to call 911," Selma instructed.

"Huh?" Kendra scrunched her face.

"We have to turn him in, Kendra," Selma said. "If we don't, we could be his next victims.

"Why don't we call the police and have them arrest him at his house?" Kendra asked.

"Baby, you need to trust me on this," Selma said.

"Remember that he is armed and dangerous, Mom," Kendra said.

"Kendra, when you grow up, you will understand certain things about men. He needs to hear this from me directly, and he needs to know that I am not afraid of him."

"He is armed, and you are not." Kendra said. "He killed his wife, and you could be next."

There was an ominous look on Tony's face as he walked into Selma's living room forty-five minutes later. He wore a pair of black sweatpants and a gray Nike fleece hoodie with a front pocket. After a quick kiss he sat on the sofa next to Selma. There was an unusual discomfort between them, and Selma wondered if he had any inkling about why she had invited him over. She cleared her throat and tightened her lips. Her heart raced as she sat next to him.

"How do you feel about me, Tony?" Selma asked.

"What do you mean?" Tony asked, showing very little emotion. "I think you are a beautiful woman, and I think I am falling in love with you." Selma took a deep breath and stared at Tony's face without speaking. "What is this all about?"

"Look me straight in the eye and call me a fool," Selma said.

"Okay, let me guess," Tony started, pulling himself closer to the edge of the sofa. "You did some investigation on me, right?" Selma did not respond. "So this is what you journalists do. You investigate and dig up stories about people."

Selma did not flinch. Tony jerked away.

"So who are you, Nelson Wright?" Selma asked. She crossed her arms and waited for Tony to respond. His head dropped, and he took a long deep breath, holding his hands together.

"I should have known," Tony said clenching his fists.

"You should have known what? I asked you a simple question."

"Now that you know, are you going to turn me in?" Tony asked. His eyes were burning red.

"No, I am not going to turn you in," Selma replied calmly. "I just want the truth."

Tony fidgeted.

"Listen, you asked, and I am going to tell you," Tony began, still feeling uneasy. He cracked his knuckles and leaned back on the sofa. Selma's eyes were fixed on him, watching his every move. "I was out there in the desert, fighting ferocious enemies." He paused and took a deep breath.

"I'm listening," Selma said.

"My wife decided to cheat on me," Tony continued. "The

dude she was having an affair with had the audacity to move into my house while I was away."

"I'm really sorry," Selma said.

"Nobody cares about us when we return from war," Tony blurted.

"Nelson, may I call you by your real name?" Selma asked.

"I knew I had PTSD, but who cared? Instead of hunting me like a wild animal, why didn't they help?"

"Nelson, I understand how much it hurts—"

"No, you don't!" Nelson sprang up from the seat and stood directly in front of Selma. "You want to write an article about a murderer you met."

"Nelson," Selma said as she stretched her hand towards him.

"Why are you calling me that?" Tony asked. "Go ahead, call the cops." He backed away and headed toward the stairs. Selma walked backward to the kitchen. Nelson charged at her and pulled a 9mm gun from his pocket.

"You don't want to do this," Selma pleaded. "Please, put the gun away." She leaned on the dining table, facing Nelson. Kendra hurried downstairs screaming. Tony turned and looked at Kendra and then at Selma.

"Please don't hurt my mom," she cried. The menacing look on his face turned desperate, and he pointed the gun first at Kendra, who was now standing behind the sofa, and then back at Selma. There was a loud knock on the door. Nelson went to the door, keeping his sights on Selma and Kendra. Selma looked across the room at her daughter but could not walk over to her. Nelson opened the front door, and stepped back. He scowled at Selma.

"I can't believe you," he mouthed.

"Drop the weapon," Officer Randal ordered, his sidearm drawn and pointed at Nelson. A second officer rushed, weapon in hand, toward Kendra. Nelson dropped the gun and glanced at Selma before surrendering to the police. The second officer quickly put on a pair of purple gloves and picked up the gun. Selma was sweating profusely as she ran to hug Kendra.

"Assailant in custody," the second officer radioed.

With Nelson in handcuffs, Selma thanked the officer. A second police cruiser was parked next to the first, the sirens on full blast. Two female officers rushed in, and one of them went to Kendra while Officer Randal pulled Selma aside to talk with her.

"Do you realize that we could have been dead tonight?" Kendra asked her mom when the officers left. Selma was still too shaken to speak.

"Let's go to bed," Selma said. "You can stay in my room if you want." Selma checked the doors and windows before she went upstairs. "Now we can actually sleep well knowing that he is in custody."

"What will happen to Latisha now?" Kendra asked Selma when they got upstairs.

"I told the police everything," said Selma. "They're going to pick her up from their house."

Selma watched Kendra as she slept in her bed. She thought about how close they had come to dying together. She knelt down and prayed.

NINETEEN

The Christmas party Selma was planning took on a new meaning. She called Julie to inform her about the dramatic arrest of Nelson Wright. Christie and Habibah were stunned to hear the news about Tony. The scary part was how close Selma had come to being his victim.

"I can't believe the risk you took," said Habibah. "And you found out about him the day we went to the doctor?" Selma nodded.

"I am just speechless," Christie said. "I'm relieved that he is in jail now."

"Julie told me that I have to press charges," Selma said.

"How about the murder he committed?" Habibah asked.

"He will be extradited to Florida eventually," Selma replied. "I can't imagine a person like him destroying his life the way he did."

"Selma, you are sounding like you feel sorry for him," Christie said.

"This is not very easy for me," Selma replied. "I saw how he snapped at my place. I imagine that he snapped like that and killed his wife." Habibah shook her head.

"I don't have any tolerance for anybody who takes the life of another person," Habibah said.

"Selma, this man is a murderer," Christie responded. "He came to your house with a gun. Can you imagine what would have happened to you and Kendra?"

"I understand the risk," Selma remarked. "Maybe it was too much of a risk, but he knew where I live. Can you imagine him showing up in the middle of the night to hurt us?"

"I would have called the police and had him arrested at his own house," Christie said.

"There was a part of me that wanted to confront him and let him know that I'm not afraid of him," Selma said defiantly.

"That was very dangerous, Selma," Habibah said. "We need to be careful with the men we let into our lives."

"You are beginning to make me feel like I brought this on myself," Selma said. Habibah placed her hand on Selma's shoulders and looked into her eyes.

"We're just scared that something terrible could have happened to you and your daughter," she said. Christie nodded. "You are one of the most intelligent women I know."

"If this could happen to you, then it could happen to others," Christie added.

"You know, you could write a column about women falling in love with a person like Tony, and finding out that he is not who he says he is," Habibah said. Selma pondered their reactions, and she understood that their responses to the incident stemmed from their love for her. Her friends cared about her, and it gave her a good feeling. She wondered how Afi would have taken the news. With Logan still in rehab, Selma had decided not to let her know about Tony. Talking to Julie was more helpful because of the legal implications. More importantly, she needed her help to prepare for court.

An hour and a half of shopping was enough to get most of the food items for the Christmas party. Selma called her brother as soon as she got home and made him promise not to tell their mother. CJ was distraught when Selma told him about Nelson. He was quiet for most of the conversation.

"And you don't want Mama to know?" he asked Selma.

"You know she will be worried, and one of us will have to make an international trip," Selma warned.

Even though she was only three years older than CJ, their parents had instilled the value of respect for elders, and CJ knew to respect his older sister at all times. They were inseparable when they were younger. CJ would threaten to fight anyone who disrespected Selma. She knew without a doubt that CJ would have confronted Nelson if he lived close by.

After speaking with her brother, Selma pulled up her internet dating article to add some finishing touches, and closed the file almost as soon as she opened it. She pondered the reactions of her friends and CJ. Nelson's story did not fit the dating article; however, she considered writing an article to tell his story, just as Habibah had suggested. Although most people who heard the news about Tony considered him a dangerous criminal, she saw it a little differently. She watched the streaming news segment on WESH, the NBC affiliate in Orlando.

The news anchor explained in great detail how Nelson attacked a local journalist, Ms. Selma Griffin, in her home. Her stomach churned when she heard her name on the news. It was a feeling she could not explain to any of her friends. In her mind, it had made sense to stay calm; asking him questions provided a window into his soul. Nelson felt betrayed and unloved, and she understood that. She thought about him as a decorated veteran who became the victim of a broken system.

But there was no justification for his actions as far as she was concerned. It bothered Selma that she had not figured it out earlier; she could not believe she had been seduced by a murderer. She thought about the men she had met online for her article, and had to reconsider the idea of online dating—or any kind of dating, for that matter. The fact that she met Tony in real life, and he turned out to be a fugitive, gave Selma a new perspective. Although the anonymity of online dating made it easy for people to assume different identities, people like Nelson could assume a different identity just to victimize others.

Selma recalled her feelings the day she went to the gym with Tony. Her admiration for him as a devoted father and as a friend had diminished, yet she struggled with the idea that the system failed him. It made sense to write an article about her short relationship with Nelson. If the only lesson her readers learned from her experience was to be vigilant when they found love, it would be a lesson worth learning. It could save lives.

Online Prince Charming Caught in a Fishing Net was published one week before Christmas. A *Gazette* graphic artist illustrated the idea of looking for love online. He created a big red heart-shaped computer monitor with lines and someone's fingers typing on the keyboard.

Cynthia was the first to congratulate Selma on the success of her column. Selma's emotions were mixed when she saw her article. As a rookie journalist writing her first investigative report, Selma felt a deep sense of accomplishment, but she recalled her first meeting with Steve Blackwell and wished he were alive to read the article.

"You are making waves, Selma," Cynthia said as she walked into Selma's office. "There are over a thousand hits online already, and it is not noon yet." Selma smiled. She noticed a card next to her phone right after Cynthia left. The handwriting was a bit sloppy, and when she opened it, she saw that it had been signed by Jeff, the newly hired reporter. Her heart skipped a beat probably because she was not expecting a card from the new employee. His face lit up when Selma stopped by his office to thank him.

"Being the new kid around here, I didn't want to be intrusive and mess anything," Jeff said. "I just want to congratulate you on the success of your column."

"Thank you, Jeff. That was very thoughtful of you." Jeff beamed. "I better let you finish your article."

"I will send you the draft within the hour," he said.

"Thanks," Selma replied and headed back to her office, the episode with Tony heavy on her mind. The only angle she could think of was that he was a war hero whose life was destroyed because he did not get the support he needed to thrive. She considered three possible headlines for her article: "The End of a Decorated Veteran," "In Love with a Fugitive," and "Tarnished Gold."

She remembered the gold earrings Eric gave her as a birthday present shortly after he proposed to her. She had not been able to believe she owned a pair of earrings made of pure gold. Selma had placed them in an old jewelry box and had not worn them since her divorce. At that moment, Tony, a.k.a. Nelson, was a golden, brave solder whose act of courage earned him a Purple Heart. He was tarnished gold.

Selma completed the draft of "Tarnished Gold" and stopped by Gary's office on her way out. Even though Gary had taken over Blackwell's editorial responsibilities, he continued to create satirical articles. Gary had just posted online a column poking fun at leaders of big polluting countries like the US lecturing poor countries about global warming.

"You have done it again, Gary!" Selma exclaimed.

"It is a dirty job, but someone has to do it," Gary joked.

"No one says it like you," Selma said. Gary sat up and looked intently at Selma.

"I do not take what happened to you lightly," Gary said. "I

have dismissed all inquiries and requests for interviews about the incident because I want you to tell your own story."

"I understand," Selma said. "I appreciate the support from all of you."

"Well, you were kind enough to invite us to your home for a Christmas party," Gary said lightheartedly. "It is the least we can do."

"I look forward to seeing you all at the party," Selma said. She closed the door behind her and headed toward the parking lot.

Kendra was sitting on the front steps with Ashley when Selma got home. Kendra walked up to her mom's car, and Ashley followed close behind.

"Hey, Mom," Kendra said.

"Are you girls warm enough in those fleece jackets?" Selma said as she stepped out of the car. Kendra wore a light blue one, and Ashley's was pink. Selma gave Kendra a hug and reached into the passenger side to get her bag.

"We are wearing sweatshirts underneath, Mom," Kendra griped.

"Hi, Ms. Griffin," Ashley said.

"Hello, Ashley," Selma replied as she gave her a side hug.

"Ashley came over to do homework with me," Kendra said as they walked to the house.

"That's nice," Selma replied. "Did you find something to eat?

"We had some Hot Pockets," Kendra replied.

"How is your mom?" Selma asked Ashley.

"She's fine," Ashley replied. Selma dropped her bag at the bottom of the staircase and walked into the kitchen. Kendra and Ashley went up to Kendra's room. After a long day at work,

Selma did not feel like cooking. She looked in the refrigerator and took out a bowl of spaghetti sauce. Boiling the spaghetti was a breeze. Ashley hesitated at first when Kendra invited her to dinner, but she gave in and had spaghetti and meatballs with Kendra and Selma.

Rosie Hinton knocked on the door just as Kendra and Ashley were clearing the plates. Selma opened the door and gave her a short embrace.

"Selma, it is so good to see you," Rosie said. She wiped her sheepskin boots on the doormat and walked in.

"Same here, Rosie," Selma said. "How have you been?"

"Fine," Rosie said. "I have been busy with Christmas shopping, and there doesn't seem to be an end in sight." Kendra and Ashley met them at the door.

"Hi, Mom."

"Hi, Mrs. Hilton," Kendra echoed.

"Are you not staying?" Selma asked Rosie who was still standing at that door.

"We should be leaving, Selma," Rosie said. "Ashley has a piano lesson in about an hour."

"Thanks for dinner, Ms. Griffin," Ashley said.

"Thank you for having Ashley," Rosie said as she adjusted her purple cashmere scarf. Kendra walked Ashley to the Lincoln Navigator. "I didn't want to say this when the girls were here, but I heard about what happened to you, and I prayed for you."

"Thank you, Rosie," Selma said. Rosie held her hands together and gazed at Selma.

"I hope you are getting the support that you need," Rosie said. "I am here for you if you need me."

"I appreciate it," Selma replied. Rosie nodded and stepped out.

"I almost forgot," Selma said. "I'm planning a Christmas party at my home, and I would like to have your family."

"Oh, thank you for inviting us," Rosie replied. "I am sorry that we will not be able to attend." Selma tried to force a smile through her tight lips.

"That's okay," Selma replied.

"We are leaving for the Bahamas on Christmas Eve," Rosie said. "We will see you when we get back."

"That's okay," Selma replied. She waited for Kendra and watched as Rosie pulled out of the parking lot.

Kendra sat on the sofa next to her mother and watched her type the events that almost took their lives.

"Mom, did you ever read or hear anything in the news about Mr. Harris?" Kendra asked.

"I did," she replied without looking up.

"Do you know what happened to Latisha?" Kendra asked. Selma stopped abruptly and placed the laptop on the coffee table.

"Kendra, I can't tell you how proud I am of you for caring about your friend," Selma said. "I was told that the Department of Social Services got involved, and they have returned her to her mother's family."

"I just want her to be okay," Kendra said. Selma leaned back on the sofa and pulled Kendra closer to her.

"I am glad we have each other," Selma said. Their tender moment was interrupted by Kendra's phone vibrating in her pocket.

"It's Ashley," she said as she removed the phone from her pocket. She gave her mother a quick kiss on the cheek and went upstairs to talk with her friend. Selma picked up her computer and continued to type her story.

TWENTY

Hosting a party two days before Christmas was a tradition Selma adopted from her parents. This Christmas party seemed like the right thing to do for her friends. She provided a box of parboiled rice, one box of grape and apple cider, a small box of malt drinks, and three packs of soda. Habibah made a trip to the international market for goat meat, tomatoes and hot pepper on Christmas morning. Although Habibah complained about the pains that she experienced at night, she refused to change anything about her lifestyle after her cancer diagnosis. Her surgery was scheduled for mid-January, and she had to take medicines to shrink the tumor. Selma invited her to spend some days with her. Habibah declined at first, but Christie persuaded her to let them take care of her. She agreed to stay with Selma for a few days while her son, Richard, stayed with Christie.

"You know how I value friendship where we come from," Christie had told Habibah.

Selma started setting the table. Christie and Richard walked in together. Richard brought two coolers for the drinks, and MJ dragged out his box of Legos and his new Star Wars Darth Vader figure. Christie placed the tray of bean cakes and fried plantains she had made for the party on the dining table.

"Merry Christmas," Christie said. "How is everything?" She placed her bag on the floor next to the sofa.

"Habibah woke up before everybody, and she has been cooking the stew," Selma replied. Habibah came out of the kitchen holding a spatula.

"Merry Christmas," she echoed.

"Good morning, Mom," Richard said as he placed the coolers on the floor. "Hi, Auntie," Richard greeted Selma. Habibah opened a bag of ice and poured it over the drinks Richard was loading into the coolers. Kendra sprinted downstairs.

"Merry Christmas to all," Kendra said.

"Where are your presents?" MJ asked Kendra.

"They're under the Christmas tree," she replied. She watched as MJ removed his Star Wars action figure from the packet.

Selma glanced at the presents under the Christmas tree in the corner. Christmas carols played in the background. Selma and Christie joined Habibah in the kitchen. The house was filled with the aroma of sautéed onions and tomatoes. Selma used a Christmas tablecloth for the dining table. She neatly arranged some of the food on the table, leaving space in the middle for a wreath and candle centerpiece. Christie and Habibah brought more food from the kitchen.

"The table looks so good," Kendra said. "Can I try something?"

"Not now," Selma replied. "We need to get ready for the party."

"I am ready," MJ called out. Everybody went upstairs to get ready, leaving MJ and Richard to watch the Christmas parade on television.

Selma noticed her phone vibrating when she got to her room. Julie was calling to say that she was running late.

Habibah came down first. She wore an embroidered, tie-dyed caftan. With her braids pulled to the side and pinned up with black hairpins, she looked as elegant as an African princess.

"Mom, you look really nice," Richard said.

"Thank you," Habibah replied. Christie and Selma came down. Christie wore a lavish lace skirt and blouse. Selma wore a silk caftan with embroidery around the neck and sleeves.

Richard opened the door for Julie. She was holding a basket containing a bottle of chardonnay, a small French cheese platter and a packet of Ritz crackers. Roberto was right behind her, holding a Whole Foods bag containing a small quesadilla platter. Richard helped them bring in the bags.

"Hello, everyone," Julie said. "I wish you all a Merry Christmas."

"Same to you," Selma, Christie and Habibah chorused.

"I know your colleagues will be here soon," Julie said. "I don't think they know about African time." Selma told Julie about African time the first time she invited Julie to her home. She explained that most of her friends came about an hour or two late to most events, and they would refer to their tardiness as African time.

"Jaden can't come," Selma said. "He told me he was going out of town."

"Well, he will miss all this good food," Christie said.

"Gary planned to stop by for a short while," Selma said.

"Did you invite the new guy?" Julie asked with a mischievous look on her face. Selma looked through her dining room window, just as Jeff was parking his red Buick Lacrosse.

"Speak of the devil," Selma said. Julie and Christie followed her gaze. Jeff got out of his car. He looked casual in jeans and a denim jacket over a long-sleeve khaki shirt. Richard opened the door for him, and took the Pyrex tray he was carrying. He placed it on the table and removed the plastic cover.

"Thanks for the shrimp and sauce, Jeff," Selma said and gave him a hug.

"Thanks for having me," Jeff said. He placed a small wrapped box under the tree. Selma watched him, admiring his confidence. His trimmed beard gave him a youthful look.

Afi and her family arrived a few minutes later. Logan was all smiles as he walked into the house holding his baby boy. Afi helped Elaine set up the cups around the ceramic punch bowl. The mood was festive, and Selma and her friends ate and drank. The door was open when Cynthia arrived wearing a green maxi dress. She placed a bag under the tree and hugged Selma. After brief introductions, Selma asked Kendra to change the music to African music.

"Just what I came for," Cynthia said. She stood up and started dancing, to the delight of Mawusi, who laughed uncontrollably. Selma and Jeff joined in. Selma urged Julie and Roberto to dance. Habibah and Christie stood and urged Logan and his family to join as well.

"Julie," Selma exclaimed as she noticed a ring on her finger. She pointed to the ring and looked at Julie. Logan sat next to his mother, holding the baby while Afi joined the ladies on the dance floor. Cynthia danced close to Julie to get a better look at the ring.

"Oops," Julie blushed. "I was going to tell you that Robby proposed." Christie's jaw dropped and she did not blink for thirty seconds. Selma hesitated at first and then congratulated Julie and Roberto. Christie tried to control her conflicted feelings of disbelief and joy. She hugged Julie and Roberto and congratulated them. Well wishes came from all corners of the room.

Richard took over from Kendra and played Beyoncé's "Single Ladies" song. Elaine and Mawusi rose to dance. Cynthia was happy to have company as she swayed her hips back and forth, mumbling words and adding other words to the lyrics.

Jeff looked through the window and noticed a shadow walking toward the house. He watched and waited. Selma turned on the porch light and saw that it was Gary. She quickly opened the door for him.

"Hello, everybody," Gary said with a grin. Kendra stopped the music and waited.

"Gary, you made it," cried Cynthia.

"I am so glad you could come, Gary," Selma said as she took his coat. "Everybody, please meet our supervisor."

"Please don't let me stop you," Gary said. "Keep dancing." He sampled the food on the table and sat next to Logan. Kendra turned on more music. Julie and Roberto stood up and danced.

"It's nice seeing you again," Logan said as Gary sat beside him. His speech was still slurred but audible. Gary smiled and tilted his head to stare at Logan.

"You must be—"

"The guy who got shot in the head," Logan interjected. Gary sat still for a few seconds, at first puzzled by Logan's response. Then he reached over and shook Logan's hand.

"It's a small world after all," Gary said. The music ended, and everybody sat down. Roberto sat on the floor next to Julie and placed his elbow on her knees. Selma sat beside Habibah. Afi beamed as she held her almost two-month-old baby. Christie smiled and placed her hand on Selma's shoulder. She stood up and thanked Selma for hosting the party and all her friends for their support. Mawusi walked to the center of the room. She glanced at everybody and made an expression in her native language. All eyes were fixed on her as if she were an oracle. She mentioned most of the food and drinks they had and thanked Selma for hosting the party.

"Friendship is a very precious gift," she said. "Between true friends even drinking water together is sweet enough." Christie nodded as Mawusi recited the African proverb. She talked about how all of Afi's friends had taken care of her since she came to the US. Logan started clapping and everyone joined in. When the clapping ended, she admonished them to treasure their friendships with one another and ended with yet another proverb: "A small house will hold a hundred friends."

There wasn't any fanfare during the gift exchange. Richard was happy to get a new cell phone. Kendra was pleased with the cosmetic kit Selma gave her. Two groups formed almost instantaneously as kids moved into the dining room with their presents and the adults stayed back and indulged in more apple cider.

"Hold a true friend with both hands," Mawusi said. Elaine gave her a hug. Julie started singing "Silent Night." Everybody sang. Gary's voice was the loudest, and off key. Baby Max was wailing when Cynthia rose to speak. Afi placed the baby on her shoulder to keep him quiet.

"On behalf of my colleagues at the *Uptown Gazette*—" Cynthia started. The baby's wailing got louder and Afi started walking around the room, trying to calm him down. "Thank you, Selma, for a very wonderful party." Jeff started the round of clapping this time.

Soon Julie and Roberto rose to leave. That started a chain of departures, with Gary and Cynthia soon heading out the door. Jeff rose and gave Selma a hug that lingered. He held her hand and whispered, "See you in the office." Christie raised an eyebrow and nudged Selma. Afi placed the baby in his carrier as Logan put a pacifier in his mouth. Elaine picked up the baby's diaper bag and headed for the door.

"Thank you for having us," Logan said as he hugged Selma on his way out.

Christie and Selma quickly put away leftovers after everybody left. Habibah sat in the sofa and leaned on the armrest. Her face contorted into a grimace as she tried to comfortably position herself. Christie helped her to stretch out.

"I think we should take you to the emergency room," Christie suggested. Habibah shook her head. Selma brought her a glass of cold water and two Advil and helped her upstairs to the guest room where she was staying. Richard followed close behind. He stood by the bed and watched his mother. With a look of trepidation on his face, he bent down and held her hand.

"Mom, you are going to be okay," he said. "You have to be okay." Habibah managed to smile, and looked at Richard.

"You have grown so quickly," she said. "I will be fine." Richard closed his eyes and two tears rolled down his face. "You listen, Richard," Habibah said. "You need to be strong for us." Richard nodded. "Stay with Auntie Christie and focus on your work and school." Richard kissed her on the forehead and left the room moments after Selma. As he walked slowly downstairs, he could hear the conversation Christie was having with Selma at the dining table.

"What a day," Christie exclaimed.

"Habibah is going to need us a lot," Selma said. "I am not going to lie—I am scared to death."

"We will pray, we will hope, and we will support Habibah as much as we can," Christie said firmly. "Life is too unfair."

"Another way to look at it is that things change," Selma said. "Look at us."

MJ came downstairs and told his mother that he was sleepy. Richard waited by the staircase.

"We will leave very soon, okay?" Christie said. MJ walked back upstairs slowly.

"Life has been good to some people even though it seems unfair to others," Selma said, philosophical. She understood how sensitive Christie could be and knew she was saying too much. "We all rallied around to help Afi and Logan, and as I watched them today I thought about their amazing triumph." Christie squeezed her lips and nodded.

"My divorce lawyer is engaged and will be getting married soon," Christie groused.

"Christie, that is life," Selma said. "Habibah is going through one of the biggest challenges, and she does not have a husband." Christie got the message.

"We are all she's got," Christie said. She soon packed up her dishes and left with MJ and Richard. Selma hugged Kendra and whispered, "I love you, Kendra."

TWENTY-ONE

The new year brought with it changes at work and at home for Selma. At the *Gazette* it was business as usual. Selma was hard at work on her column about Nelson. She thought about the subpoena she had received the day before to testify at the preliminary hearing of Nelson's case. Writing about how the system had failed Nelson, a man charged with attempting to kill her, did seem counterintuitive, but she stuck to her principle.

Selma opened a new document and wrote a statement for the prosecution outlining reasons for the case to be dropped so that Nelson could be extradited to Florida to face the murder charge in the death of his wife. After a quick review, she sent it as an email attachment to the lead prosecutor.

Selma sent a lead to Jeff for an article on how local residents were bracing for the impending storm that was headed toward the Mid-Atlantic region. Her focus was to complete her column article on Nelson in time for Jaden to edit it before the end of the day. Jeff walked into her office before Selma realized that he was there.

"I'm sorry I came in without knocking," Jeff said.

"I have been wrapped up in this article," Selma began.

"I totally understand," Jeff said. "That's why I'm here."

There was a breaking news story from the Associate Press streaming in about the arrest of a lawyer in Manhattan; Selma ignored it. She fidgeted and sat up straight.

"I really appreciate your understanding," Selma said. "There is so much to do in so little time in this business."

"I know exactly what you mean," Jeff said and paused for a few seconds. "First, I'd like to thank you for hosting that wonderful Christmas party." Selma gazed at him. "Second, you seem like you could use a friend."

"What do you mean? I have friends. What are you really saying?"

"You have amazing friends, and you are doing so much and giving so much of yourself." Jeff stopped briefly when he noticed the stern look on Selma's face. "I wish you would give me a chance to be there for you as well." He stepped back and waited for a response.

"Listen, I am sitting here writing an article about a big mistake I made," Selma replied. "I appreciate what you are doing, but I think it's best if we focus on our work here."

"I understand," Jeff said, bowing his head in defeat as he quietly left.

"The nerve," Selma whispered to herself. She looked at the three titles that she had scribbled on a note card and underlined "Tarnished Gold."

Gary rushed into Selma's office using hand gestures to tell Selma to read the article that was streaming.

"I saw it, but I have so much on my plate right now," she said.

"Read it, *now*," Gary said firmly. It was a side of Gary she had not seen before. She opened the article and her jaw dropped and eyes widened. "Now you see why." Selma turned and stared at Gary. She read the first two lines out loud.

"A female lawyer from Nigeria and her accomplice, Martin Chinedu, were arrested at LaGuardia airport this morning and charged with racketeering and illegal transfer of funds to Nigeria."

"That is your friend, right?" Gary said.

"Absolutely not!" Selma exclaimed. "Well, he is my friend's estranged husband."

"Well, I'm sorry," Gary said. "There is more; do you want to continue reading?" Selma read the next paragraph and dropped her head on her desk. Gary placed his hand on her shoulder.

"I can't believe what I'm reading," Selma said. She raised her head up and read the second sentence loudly.

"Investigators have uncovered the couple's elaborate scheme to hire a hit man to kill Mr. Chinedu's estranged wife and abduct his son. Among the items found in their possession is a passport belonging Mr. Chinedu's son, Martin Jr." Selma bit her lower lip and took a deep breath.

"This must be hard to swallow," Gary said. "I know this is your good friend. I better leave you alone to think about what you want to do."

Selma finished reading the story and saved it. Her mind went to the upcoming custody hearing. Her first instinct was to call Julie, but her call went to voicemail. She tried Christie next.

"Hey, Christie, could you come by my house when you get off work?" Selma said

"Yes," she replied. "Is Habibah okay?"

"She's resting and getting ready for tomorrow," Selma replied.

She could tell from Christie's response that she had not seen or read the article. She pondered the serendipitous news and the impact it would have on her friend. She printed the entire article and placed it in a manila folder and then went to see Jaden.

"I cannot send you my column today," Selma said when she got to his office. The distress on her face was obvious.

"Is everything alright?" he asked. Selma nodded as she held in her lips. "Send it when you can; you know there is no rush."

"Cynthia has it now," Selma said. "I could use her input."

"Not a problem, Selma," Jaden replied. Just let me know how I can help."

"Thanks," Selma said and went back to her office.

There was a text and a missed call from Julie when Selma got back to her office. She called her again and this time she answered.

"I was in court when you called," Julie said. "What's going on?"

"Julie, I need you to stop by my house after work, please," Selma said.

"Okay."

Julie got to Selma's house less than thirty minutes after Selma got home. Kendra was typing her homework assignment on her laptop and munching on pizza bites.

"Habibah is upstairs, and I have not told her anything," Selma said as Julie walked into her living room. Kendra raised her head and gazed at her mother, hoping to get a gist of what she was talking about. "Kendra, could you excuse Ms. Julie and me for a few minutes." Kendra grabbed her computer and stuffed the two pizza bites that she had placed on a napkin in her mouth.

"Well, at least I know you did not get a call from school about me today," Kendra said with a mouth full of pizza. She meandered up the stairs to her room. Christie knocked on the door, and Selma hurried to open it while Julie made herself comfortable on the sofa.

"I'm sorry for dragging you here, but this is something that you both need to know," Selma said as she handed the manila folder to Julie. Christie looked at Selma and then at Julie, trying to figure out what the issue was.

"This is unreal!" Julie exclaimed as she read. "I can't believe this."

"Believe what?" Christie asked.

"Listen," Selma began. "Martin has been arrested in New York."

"What did he do?" Christie asked.

"He and his girlfriend were caught stealing money from various organizations and sending it to Nigeria. They also found out that he was plotting to kill you and kidnap MJ."

Christie sat transfixed for almost a minute. No one spoke. Tears flowed.

"Christie, I am very sorry."

"So, he really hated me that much?" Christie cried.

"We are preparing for the custody hearing, and people like Martin do these types of things to avoid paying child support," Julie said.

"The good thing is that he is arrested," Selma said. "He will not hurt you again."

"He has made our case easy because he will not be appearing in court," Julie said.

"So I would have been killed just because of child custody and child support," Christie said. "I see these stories on TV, and I never think of anything like that happening to me."

"We have to thank Selma for helping us find out," Julie said. "I am sure that the story is streaming all over the media."

"God works in mysterious ways," Selma said. Julie rose to leave.

"Thank you for the tip, Selma," Julie said. "I should be leaving now." She stuck the manila folder in her bag and headed for the door. Christie waved goodbye and remained seated, still in shock.

"Now I am in fear for my life," Christie said.

"He's in jail," Selma said.

"How about the person he hired to kill me?" Christie said. Selma could sense Christie's trepidation as she spoke.

"Remember what I said earlier about how God works in mysterious ways," Selma said as she sat next to Christie. "You will be fine. Remember that he got caught, and now he has to face the consequence of his action. This is one of those rare miracles that happen when God is looking out for you."

"That's true," Christie responded.

"You and your son are safe," Selma said. "He will not be able to carry out his awful plans to harm you and your son." Christie nodded and gave Selma a hug before leaving.

Selma was in a jovial mood when she got to the office the next day. After staying up to finish her article, she was ready to send it to Jaden. Selma had already outlined her next article, which would be about the obstacles women faced when going through the divorce process. Selma made a quick stop at Jeff's office.

"Knock, knock," Selma said to get his attention. Jeff leaned back and smiled.

"Good morning, Selma," he replied. "You seem to be in a better mood this morning."

"I'm sorry for acting silly yesterday," Selma said. "I saw the final draft of the snowstorm article, and I like your attention to details about its impact on the metro system." Jeff smiled.

"Thank you," Jeff said.

"Jeff, you are an experienced journalist," Selma said. "You can handle any article."

"Well, thanks for your vote of confidence," Jeff said. "I am starting the article about Super Bowl XLIV predictions and the *fandomanium* involved!"

"That sounds exciting," Selma said. "I may not be able to work with you on it today because I have to leave early."

"I got this," Jeff replied.

"Jaden will alert you to any breaking news," Selma said. "Well, let me go and see the boss."

"I have a card for you, Selma," Jeff said as he handed her a card addressed to Ms. Griffin in purple ink.

"Thanks," Selma said and hurried to Gary's office.

"Good morning, Gary," Selma said as she stepped in.

"Great to see you in a cheerful mood," Gary said. He sat up and gave Selma a look of subtle inquiry.

"I have talked to my friends about the arrest, and they have a handle on it," Selma responded.

"Your 'Tarnished Gold' column article is headed for publication," Gary replied.

"Thank you, Gary," Selma said. "I have to take my friend to see her oncologist."

"I hope and pray for the very best," Gary said.

Habibah wore a long skirt and blouse made from a festive green African print fabric. She wore a green *hijab* to match the fabric.

"You look really nice," Selma said. "You're really dressed up for this doctor's appointment."

"I decided to dress up today because I may not be doing a lot of it," Habibah said nonchalantly.

"You need to stop talking like that," Selma said. "You will have the rest of your life to dress up and be the beauty queen you are."

"Well, since you are curious, this *hijab* was my mother's favorite," Habibah said. "I am wearing it today because I want to feel close to her." Selma cast an incredulous look at her. "You know this has nothing to do with religion, right?"

"I know your stance on religion, and I have always respected that," Selma replied. "We better leave now; I don't want you to be late."

It was a forty-five-minute ride to Georgetown Hospital. Habibah and Selma did not speak for almost ten minutes.

"Selma, I really appreciate you taking me to my appointment," Habibah said.

"I'm glad to do it, Habibah," Selma replied. "You would do it for any of us." There was silence for another five minutes.

"One side effect of the medicine I'm taking is hair loss," Habibah said. "I have been losing some of my hair. I'll be using my *hijab* a lot to cover it."

"This is journey, Habibah, and we are going to be there with you every step of the way," Selma said. "Christie told you that she plans to take off from work on the day of your surgery, right?"

"Yes," Habibah replied in a faint voice.

"We are all here for you, and we are rooting for you, Habibah," Selma reassured her.

"I appreciate everything you all are doing for me."

"You know you would do the same for any of us," Selma repeated as she drove through the parking lot looking for an empty space. When they walked into the office, Habibah whispered to Selma to stay in the waiting room when she got called.

"I will ask for you when the doctor tells me what I need to do next," Habibah whispered.

"Fine."

Habibah's oncologist, Dr. Lynn Snyder, sat on the stool across the exam table and skimmed through the reports. She talked with Habibah about the need for surgery.

"There are no assurances," Dr. Snyder said. "But I believe that surgery and radiation will give you a good chance for remission."

"I am ready," Habibah replied.

"You indicated a history of breast cancer," Dr. Snyder said, flipping through Habibah's records.

"My mother died of breast cancer," Habibah replied.

"You have a chance, and we are going to do everything we can for you," Dr. Snyder responded. "I will contact our surgeon to schedule your surgery right away." She examined Habibah for about ten minutes before sending her to the lab and radiologist for some blood tests and an X-ray.

Selma was relieved to see Habibah smile when she came into the waiting room.

"There is hope," Habibah said. Selma patted her on the back and they walked toward to elevator.

Habibah fell asleep during the ride home, but she was wide awake when they arrived. Habibah called Christie and told her about her doctor's visit.

The week following Habibah's first doctor's visit turned into a wild, unending rollercoaster ride for Selma. The four-inch snowfall that hit the region impacted her morning commute to work. Habibah stayed in the guest room most of the time, reading and preparing herself mentally for surgery. Although Kendra did not like the idea of Habibah spending a long time at their home, she was glad to have her there when she stayed home during two snow days.

With one week before Habibah's lumpectomy, Selma worked on the article for her column, which she titled "Turning Point." Habibah did not mind being the focus. The publication of "Tarnished Gold" got a lot of attention, and most of the people who responded sympathized with Selma. Some readers responded to the call for better care for veterans. The news of Nelson's arrest had gone viral and attracted the attention of cable news and NBC Nightly news. Jaden informed Selma that Dateline NBC was working on an investigative report on the story. Selma was not sure she was ready for that kind of attention, but she felt good to know that her article had such an impact.

Selma wanted to complete the "Turning Point" article before Habibah's surgery, and stayed up several nights to work on it. Habibah contributed to the article by telling Selma how her cancer diagnosis had become a turning point in her life. It had a bigger meaning for her because her mother did not survive. Selma wrote about the impact of cancer on families, careers and relationships.

Habibah waited for Christie on the morning of her surgery. Selma had to go to the office, but planned to meet them at the hospital. The surgery went as planned, and Habibah spent a night at the hospital. Dr. Snyder came to see Habibah shortly before she was discharged and assured her that the lump had been successfully removed, and she would start radiation the following week. Christie and Selma decided that it was best for Habibah to stay with Selma.

Christie's court case turned out not to be as eventful as anticipated. Afi had taken off work to go with Christie. With Martin still awaiting trial for his criminal case in New York, his attorney presented Martin's case in court. He was requesting full custody of MJ, the family's house, and child support from Christie. Julie, representing Christie, showed a pattern of verbal, emotional, and physical abuse that made Martin unfit to have custody of their son. The arrest and incarceration of Martin and his mistress for racketeering made the judge's decision easy.

Christie was awarded full custody of MJ and ownership of the house, plus garnishment of any money Martin had to be used for child support and alimony.

When Selma got home from work that day, she reflected on the events of the past few weeks, and sat at the dining table looking out the window. She was thankful that she had all her Saturday mornings back after resigning from Montgomery College. Her brother had traveled to Nigeria to bring her mother to visit. The following morning was peaceful when Selma went to the kitchen to boil water for tea. She heard Habibah's sobbing and rushed upstairs to check on her. "Habibah," Selma called frantically. She peeked into the room and saw her sitting on the floor and weeping.

"What is the matter?" Selma asked

"It hurts so much," Habibah replied.

"It will be okay," Selma reassured her. "You will get through this."

"What if I don't?" Habibah asked. Selma saw the desperate look on her face and broke down and cried with her.

"The worst part is dying here, far from home, Selma," Habibah cried.

"You are not going to die, you hear me." Selma held Habibah's face in her hand and looked in her eyes. "Your son is here, and you have friends who care about you deeply." She could not bear to see Habibah's face contorted into a grimace. "You will face this with courage, and you will fight this thing with every ounce of strength you have." Habibah clung to Selma's shoulders and sobbed until she dozed off. Selma raised her gently and got her to lie in bed, her eyes facing the ceiling.

Selma walked away quietly. She looked into Kendra's room

and saw her fast asleep. She tiptoed downstairs and made some English breakfast black tea. She grabbed the paper that she had left on the coffee table and went to the dining room, where she sat at her favorite spot facing the window. The *Gazette* was opened to her column. She had placed the card she received from Jeff on the table next to the paper. The graphic placed above the byline was appealing.

Selma read the first part of the story and got chills as she read the events that had taken place the night Nelson was arrested at her house. She decided to drop the paper and read Jeff's card. *We travel different roads; sometimes they diverge in the yellow wood, and sometimes they cross. I don't know why our paths have crossed, but I hope you will give us a chance to figure it out together. You are a remarkable woman.*

She could not believe the metaphors he used to get her attention. For the first time since she had met him, she thought about the kind of man he was. Her mind went back to her article. She could not understand why she was so forgiving of Nelson. The fact that he killed the mother of his own child haunted her.

Through the window, she caught a glimpse of the rising sun behind a bank of bright yellow and orange clouds and took a sip of her tea. For what it was worth, it was a new day dawning.

ACKNOWLEDGMENTS

I would like to express my profound gratitude to my daughter, Nneka, who inspired the title of this story. I cannot express enough thanks to my friends for their continued support and encouragement. I am blessed to have friends who have shared my pains as well as my happiness. Thanks to my friend, Richard Waver, for encouraging me to finish this story. Thank you to my colleague, Professor Mary Hartig, for reading and editing my first draft.

Special thanks to Dr. Funso Afolayan, who has supported me. Thank you for taking on the task of reading and reviewing the story. I hope I made you and Bola proud.

And thanks to my colleagues at Montgomery College, Dr. Patrick Thomas, Professor Mary Hartig, and Professor Ruth Markulis for your endorsements. My special thanks to Dr. Mary Owens for her endorsement.

I am highly indebted to John Koehler for believing in me. My special thanks to Joe Coccaro and the editing team for paying attention to details making this story a great read.

CPSIA information can be obtained
at www.ICGtesting.com
Printed in the USA
BVHW03s2148181018
530670BV00001B/33/P

9 781633 935853